D1637880

ONE WILD WEEKEND

"Saved by the Bell" titles include:

Mark-Paul Gosselaar: Ultimate Gold
Mario Lopez: High-Voltage Star
Behind the Scenes at "Saved by the Bell"
Beauty and Fitness with "Saved by the Bell"
Dustin Diamond: Teen Star

▲　　▼　　▲

Hot new fiction titles:

Zack Strikes Back
Bayside Madness
California Scheming
Girls' Night Out
Zack's Last Scam
Class Trip Chaos
That Old Zack Magic
Impeach Screech!
One Wild Weekend

ONE WILD WEEKEND

by Beth Cruise

Collier Books
Macmillan Publishing Company *New York*
Maxwell Macmillan Canada *Toronto*
Maxwell Macmillan International
New York Oxford Singapore Sydney

Collier Books
Macmillan Publishing Company
866 Third Avenue
New York, NY 10022

Maxwell Macmillan Canada, Inc.
1200 Eglinton Avenue East
Suite 200
Don Mills, Ontario M3C 3N1
Macmillan Publishing Company is part of the Maxwell Communication
Group of Companies.
First Collier Books edition 1993
Printed in the United States of America
10 9 8 7 6 5 4 3 2 1
ISBN 0-02-042763-8

To Franco Bario

ONE WILD WEEKEND

Chapter 1

▲   ▼   ▲   ▼   ▲

"*Countdown,*" Zack Morris muttered under his breath. He stared at his watch as Mr. Loomis, the toughest history teacher at Bayside High, droned on about something historical.

There was only one minute left until the final bell. At last, the long school day was over. It was time to live again!

It was a gorgeous spring day in Palisades, California, and Zack's only problem was how to spend the rest of the afternoon. At the Max, the school hangout, eating nachos? At the beach, catching waves? At the tennis courts, hitting balls to the prettiest girl at Bayside High, Kelly Kapowski?

Tennis was a definite possibility, Zack decided. There was nothing like a tiny little white tennis dress to cheer up a fellow after the most boring history class in, well, history.

"Mr. Morris?" Mr. Loomis said icily. "If you can *possibly* tear your eyes away from your wrist, would you mind explaining to the class the significance of the Sherman Antitrust Act?"

"Sure, Mr. Loomis," Zack said, flashing his confident grin. There were fifty long seconds until the bell, and he had no idea what the answer was. But Zack Morris never let a little lack of knowledge stop him from posing as an expert. All he had to do was stall, and he'd be saved by the bell.

Zack put on his studious look. "Personally, Mr. Loomis, I'm fascinated by the Sherman Antitrust Act. It was very...significant."

"The question was *why*, Mr. Morris," Mr. Loomis said. His thick eyebrows came down in a menacing way. *Poor Mr. Loomis*, Zack thought. *He just doesn't know how to lighten up.*

"Well, because it was antitrust," Zack explained. *Forty-five seconds.* "And trusts were a very big deal in the old days. Think of the whole trust thing like...Madonna."

"Madonna," Mr. Loomis repeated dubiously.

"Exactamente," Zack said. "Those trusts involved mondo bucks. They were conglomerates. Industries unto themselves. If there was a *People* magazine back then, they'd be on the cover. Like Madonna."

"I guess that's one way of looking at it," Mr. Loomis said.

Thirty seconds. Twenty-nine... "Personally, I think old Sherman was real courageous," Zack added. "Taking on the trusts—wow. It would be like...Trish Yardley and the Slickers taking on Madonna." Trish Yardley and the Slickers was a local girl group that played at the Bayside High dances.

Mr. Loomis gave a sour smile. "A brilliant summary, Mr. Morris—"

"Thank you," Zack said modestly. *Ten seconds. Nine...*

"—that managed to contain not one fact," Mr. Loomis boomed. "Have you read the material?"

"Yes, Mr. Loomis," Zack said sincerely. "And I found it *fascinating*. Really."

Brrrrinnng! The last bell clanged, and Zack shut his history book with a snap. All *right!* He smoothed back his blond hair and flashed a grin at Kelly, who was sitting across the room. She shook her head ruefully at him, her deep blue eyes concerned. Kelly was a sweet, by-the-book kind of girl, but he was nuts about her, anyway.

As Zack hurried to catch up with Kelly at the door, he passed Mr. Loomis's desk. Suddenly, Zack felt a strong hand grasp his shoulder.

"Are you aware, Mr. Morris, that your *C* minus average is heading straight into *D* territory?"

"I *have* given it some thought," Zack said. "I'll try harder, Mr. Loomis."

Mr. Loomis snapped his briefcase shut. "Just make sure you succeed, or your parents will arrive at graduation and wonder why their son isn't wearing a cap and gown."

Zack swallowed. "Got ya, Mr. Loomis."

Bummer, Zack thought. Flunking history was not in his plans for a stress-free existence. But a glance out the window restored his good mood. Sunlight sparkled on the chrome of his white convertible Mustang. He had the car, he had the haircut, he had the perfect spring day. All he needed was the girl.

He found Kelly standing by the lockers, talking to their friends. "Everything okay with Loomis?" she asked in a low tone.

"Piece of cake," Zack said. Kelly would worry too much if she found out he was in danger of flunking. She wouldn't be *surprised,* but she'd be worried.

"I say we head for the beach this afternoon," Jessie Spano said as she loaded her arms with books from her locker. "I've got some reading to do, and I might as well get a tan while I do it."

A. C. Slater groaned. "Leave it to Jessie to treat a beach like a library." His dimples deepened and his warm brown eyes twinkled as he grinned at her. "But, then again, I totally approve of her doing homework in a bikini."

Jessie tossed her long, curly hair. "There's more to life than bikinis, Slater."

"Sure," Slater said. "Miniskirts!"

Slater and Jessie were such opposites that the gang considered it incredible that they had managed to get together at all. Jessie was studious and politically correct. She considered macho Slater a caveman with dimples. Slater had more knock-down-and-drag-outs with Jessie than he did as quarterback of the Bayside football team and captain of the wrestling team combined.

"The beach sounds good to me," Kelly said.

"I was thinking about tennis," Zack said. "But volleyball at the beach would be cool."

"I hope not *too* cool," Samuel "Screech" Powers said. He shivered violently, his frizzy curls bobbing. "I didn't bring my sweatshirt."

"No, Screech," Kelly said patiently as she swung a lock of silky dark hair behind her shoulder. "Zack meant it would be *fun.*"

"As long as you're not on my team," Slater said under his breath. With Screech's skinny, hyperactive body and total lack of concentration, he was not the greatest volleyball player. He would get distracted by a sea gull or something and accidentally send the ball halfway to Japan.

"So let's go," Jessie said.

"We're there," Slater agreed.

"No, we're not, Slater," Screech explained. "We're still at Bayside High."

Lisa Turtle heaved an enormous sigh. The pretty African-American teen had been standing by silently. And it wasn't like Lisa not to join in when leisure time was the topic under discussion.

"You guys are so mean," she said, her big brown eyes sorrowful. "Your hearts are made of concrete. Cold, hard, pebbly concrete."

"Not mine, Lisa," Screech said, placing a hand over his heart. "When it comes to you, it's made of really sticky goo." It was true. Lisa was Screech's idea of the perfect girl. He was positive that one day she'd realize that he was her perfect mate. Until then, she'd keep deluding herself that she was in love with other guys. Poor Lisa. She actually thought that being the dating queen of Bayside High was *fun*.

"Doesn't anybody remember I have to work this afternoon?" Lisa moaned. "I just *hate* it when work interferes with life."

"I thought you were starting to like being a candy striper, Lisa," Kelly said sympathetically.

"Well, I was," Lisa sniffed. "The uniform *is* really adorable. Especially since I shortened the skirt to the perfect length. And I *do* like to talk to some of the patients—especially if they're young and cute. But it's been so awful lately. You can't believe what Nurse Moore expects me to do!" Lisa's pretty brown eyes grew even wider in horror.

"What?" Jessie breathed.

"Work!" Lisa wailed.

"Whoa," Zack said. "I'd report that Moore person to the nurses' union if I were you."

"You don't understand, Zack," Lisa said. "There's a nurse shortage at the hospital, so I've been working extra hard. I didn't even get to take my break yesterday. Can you believe it? I walked around all afternoon without freshening my lipstick!"

"Horrors!" Slater said.

"I hate it when that happens," Zack agreed, and the two boys guffawed.

Jessie swung her long, curly hair behind her shoulder. "If you hate it so much, Lisa, why don't you quit?" she suggested logically.

"Get real," Lisa said with a sigh. "My parents would freak." Lisa's parents were both doctors at Palisades General. "They're still hoping I'll drop my interest in a fashion career and go to medical school."

"Maybe they'll build a new wing of Palisades General at the mall," Slater said. "That way, you could combine both of your interests." He laughed at his own joke.

"Dr. Lisa," Zack said musingly. "Wait, I can see it now." Pursing his lips, he held out an imaginary garment by an imaginary hanger. "I'm sorry, nurse, but this surgical gown just won't do. Green is *not* my color."

Everyone burst out laughing. Lisa was ultrafeminine and fervently believed that the route to world peace was paved with washable silk. If everyone would just concentrate on developing a good fashion sense, they wouldn't have time to disagree, and the world would be so much prettier! She might even consider watching the evening news.

"I can see it now," Jessie said, still laughing. She put on an announcer's voice: "Today, Dr. Lisa will lecture on the importance of moisturizer after a trip to the solarium."

Kelly giggled. "Attention, nurses. Dr. Lisa has organized a strike for better shoes!"

Slater put on a fretful expression. "But, nurse, I *can't* do the operation now!" he wailed, waggling his fingers. "My nails aren't dry!"

Everyone laughed even harder. Lisa laughed along with them, but in her opinion, her friends didn't have to laugh *quite* so long. The jokes weren't *that* funny.

Even though she'd just been complaining, Lisa knew she was good at her job. She had come in first in her first-aid training class, and she found medicine kind of fascinating. But no one saw her as a serious person, and they'd probably laugh at her even harder if they knew that she didn't think her parents' dream was completely out of the question.

Lisa frowned as Zack and Slater gave each other a high five and Kelly and Jessie wiped tears from their eyes. No, if today was any indication, she'd never breathe a word about actually wanting to become Dr. Lisa. She'd be the laughingstock of Bayside High!

▲   ▼   ▲

Kelly decided to ride with Jessie to the beach, so Zack headed for his car by himself. The parking lot had practically cleared out. On a day like today, no student wanted to hang out inside school.

Zack paused as he noticed a green sticker plastered on his rear bumper. He frowned as he read GREEN TEENS LOVE TREES. *Jessie*, he thought with a weary sigh. Zack would never spoil the pristine beauty of the world's greatest automobile. But when it came to the environment, Jessie didn't even allow a Mustang to get in her way.

Zack slid into the driver's seat. He revved the engine, checked the rearview mirror, and stepped on the gas. Since there were no other cars around, he pulled out faster than he normally would. He turned the wheel to the right, and the Mustang responded instantly with a surge of power.

Crash! Zack hit the brakes as the car shook and he heard the sickening sound of metal shrieking against metal. What could he have backed into? The spaces around him were empty!

Shakily, Zack slid out of the car and walked to the rear. Slid under his rear wheel was what had once been a pristine Harley-Davidson motorcycle. Now it was twisted, as if it were in agony. The shiny paint job was scratched, and red flakes were scattered on the pavement.

Major bummer, Zack thought, grimacing. It looked like the bike was totaled. He couldn't believe he hadn't seen it! Sighing, Zack reached into the backseat and tore off a sheet of notebook paper so that he could write down his name and number. The poor goofball who owned it was going to flip when he saw it.

Suddenly, a jolt of pure, unadulterated panic raced through Zack. He froze, the white paper waving in the slight breeze. He had just realized who the poor goofball was. And he *wasn't* a poor goofball at all. He was the biggest hood at Bayside High, Denny Vane!

Denny was six feet worth of wiry muscle and bad attitude. He clomped through Bayside High in black leather and boots, even during the hottest days. Everybody, even linebacker Butch Henderson, steered clear of him. And Denny's motorcycle was his pride and joy.

A sickening feeling gripped Zack's stomach as he looked down at the smashed, twisted bike. The sight would be nothing compared with what *Zack* would look like when Denny found out.

Quickly, he crumpled up the piece of paper and tossed it into the backseat. He might be clumsy, but he wasn't crazy. Denny could never find out that it had been Zack Morris who had destroyed the hood's reason for living. He'd twist him up like a pretzel.

Zack furtively scanned the area. There was

no one in the parking lot. No one was standing at a window in the school building. No one was kicking around a football on the field across the lot. The coast was clear for the quickest getaway since Bonnie and Clyde.

Zack leaped back into his car and threw it into drive. He stepped on the gas hard, and his car rolled over the bike with an awful crunching sound. He bumped over the grass divider into the next lane. Then, tires squealing, Zack peeled out of the parking lot. The nightmare was behind him. He was safe!

Chapter 2

▲　▼　▲　▼　▲

By the time Lisa had fought traffic, changed into her candy striper uniform, and applied matching lipstick, she was late for her shift. Even though she was only a little late, she was in trouble because Nurse Moore had a stopwatch for a brain.

Lisa had gotten on Nurse Moore's bad side on her very first day when she'd oh-so-tactfully suggested that the powder blue cardigan Nurse Moore was wearing over her white nurse's uniform was making her skin tone just the teensiest bit green. A warm rose would have really made a difference. You'd think that Nurse Moore would have been grateful! Instead, she'd assigned Lisa to bedpan duty.

Lisa hurried down the hall, her heart pounding. She prayed she wouldn't run into Nurse Moore. She'd go straight to the solarium and check to make sure that the books and magazines were neatly arranged. Nurse Moore hated a mess.

"Miss Turtle! You're late!"

Lisa stopped. Without even turning, she knew who that sharp voice belonged to. She sighed and turned around. Nurse Moore motioned her over behind the nurses' station.

"I know I'm a little late, Nurse Moore. I'm sorry," Lisa said as she came up. "I hit some traffic on the way, and—"

"Never mind that now," Nurse Moore said. "I need to tell you about the new patient in three thirteen. Buck Wintergreen is here for a hernia operation. I want you to take very special care of him."

Lisa nodded, confused. Hernia operations were pretty routine. Why did she have to fuss over the new patient? "I'll do my best, Nurse Moore."

Nurse Moore's thin lips pressed together. "You'll need to do better than your best, Miss Turtle. Mr. Wintergreen is on the hospital board. He is a VIP patient. When he says jump, you say how high and out which window. Got that?"

Lisa nodded. "Got it. I'll take extra special care of..." What was his name again? Lisa wondered. Something to do with Life Savers. "...uh, Mr. Pep-o-mint."

Nurse Moore closed her eyes. "Winter-green," she said through clenched teeth.

"Right. That's what I said. Wintergreen," Lisa repeated.

"Now get the magazine cart and bring it to Room three-thirteen," Nurse Moore ordered. "And make sure you have current issues!"

Lisa hurried away down the corridor. She found the magazine cart in the solarium and arranged the most current issues on top. Then she pushed it down the hall to Room 313.

A burly, white-haired man lay in a hospital bed. His thick white eyebrows were drawn over his sharp black eyes in a deep scowl. "Who's that?" he barked.

"Don't panic, it's not a doctor. Just a candy striper," Lisa said cheerily as she pushed the cart alongside the bed. "I'm Lisa, Mr. Wintergreen. I thought you might like some reading material this afternoon."

"I have my own reading material, young lady," Buck Wintergreen said. He looked down at the cart. "And *Pregnancy Today* is not my idea of fascinating reading, either."

Lisa quickly tucked the magazine under a newsmagazine that was three weeks old. "Can I get you anything else?" she asked, determinedly keeping a cheerful note in her voice.

"You can help me move this dang bed tray," Mr. Wintergreen said. He swatted at the bed tray that was attached by a long metal arm to one side of the bed.

"I'd be happy to." Lisa reached over to swing the bed tray to one side. She'd done it a thousand times. But this time, it stuck. Lisa yanked at it. "I've almost got it," she said brightly.

"Just watch out for the—"

But with Lisa's final yank, the pitcher of ice water flew off the tray and ended up on Mr. Wintergreen's pajamas. He flew upright in shock, letting out a yell that rattled the blinds.

"Oh, dear!" Lisa wrung her hands. "Oh, gosh! I'm so sorry." She reached for a towel on the night table and knocked over the full glass. It spilled on Mr. Wintergreen's pillow. "Oh, shoot! Gosh! I'm sorry."

"You—incompetent—nincompoop!"   Mr. Wintergreen bellowed between gasps.

"Are you in pain?" Lisa asked. "Let me help you. Should I call a nurse?"

"Get—out!" Mr. Wintergreen gasped. He tried to wipe off the ice water with his blanket.

The door opened, and Nurse Moore ran in. "Whatever is going on here? Mr. Wintergreen?" She reached for his wrist to read his pulse. "Are you all right?"

Mr. Wintergreen snatched his wrist out of her grasp. "I'm fine. I'm just freezing to death, thanks to that...that—"

"Incompetent nincompoop," Lisa supplied faintly.

Nurse Moore turned and fixed Lisa with her beady gaze. "Out, Miss Turtle. I'll see you at the nurses' station as soon as I get Mr. Wintergreen fixed up. Oh, and tell housekeeping to bring some clean linens in here, stat."

Stat meant quicker than immediately. Lisa ran out of the room and hurried to the phone. She dialed the right extension, gave the order, and then dropped her head in her hands. She knew what was in store for the rest of the afternoon. Bedpan City.

▲ ▼ ▲

That evening, Zack sat at the kitchen table while his mother bustled around the kitchen. He stared at his open history book and thought about Denny while his mother pulled things out of the refrigerator for dinner. She tied an apron around her suit and kicked off her pumps as she peered at the label on a plastic container.

"I can't tell whether this is enchiladas or clam chowder," she muttered. "Oh, well. They both go with chicken."

The phone rang, and she picked it up. "Oh, hi, Kelly. Yes, he's right here, sweetie." She handed the phone to Zack. "I'm going upstairs to change."

Zack nodded and took the phone. As soon as he heard Kelly's icy voice, he knew he was in trouble. Could she have found out about his hit-and-run experience?

"Hi, Kelly," he said in a too-cheerful voice.

"How's it going?" There was a short silence. "Is everything okay?"

"No, everything is *not* okay," Kelly said. "And I think you know why."

"I do?" Zack stalled. How could Kelly have found out?

"Zack, I waited at the beach for you until five o'clock," Kelly said. "How could you stand me up like that?"

The beach! He'd completely forgotten that he was supposed to meet Kelly there. He'd been so nervous about driving the Mustang around that he'd immediately headed for his house and put the car in the garage. If someone had seen a white Mustang peel out of the Bayside High parking lot, it wouldn't take Denny long to figure out who'd creamed his bike. And then there was the telltale dent and the red paint on his bumper.

"Kelly, I'm so sorry," he said rapidly, trying to think. He couldn't tell Kelly the truth. Kelly was too honest. She'd tell him to do the right thing and go over to Denny's house to confess. Zack hated doing the right thing. It was so...inconvenient.

"I was just going to call you," he said. "Whew. I just got home myself. My car broke down right on the freeway! It was a nightmare." Luckily, Zack's mother had left the kitchen. If she heard him telling Kelly such a big lie, she'd ground him for fifty years *and* tell Kelly the truth.

Kelly's tone instantly melted into concern. "Zack, that's awful. Are you okay? Breaking down on the freeway can be really dangerous."

"I'm fine," Zack said quickly. "I lucked out and pulled off right near a phone. I had the car towed to my mechanic's. He's not sure what's wrong, though." This was perfect, Zack thought. Now he wouldn't have to take the car to school tomorrow. He could keep it in the garage until he was positive the coast was clear.

"Zack, I'm really sorry," Kelly said. "If you need money to fix it, I can lend you some from my college fund."

Zack winced. Sometimes it was hard having such a nice girlfriend. The guilt quotient could soar dangerously high. "That's really sweet of you, Kelly, but, no," he said. "I can handle it. But I can't pick you up for school tomorrow."

"That's okay," Kelly said. "I can hitch a ride from my older brother. I'm about to call Jessie. Do you want me to ask her if you can ride with Slater and her?"

"That would be great," Zack said. "Thanks." He wished that Kelly would stop doing him favors. It made him feel twice as guilty for lying to her.

He hung up just as his mother came back into the kitchen, now dressed casually in jeans. "Honey, can you do me a favor?" she asked. "I forgot to pick up my allergy prescription at the drugstore.

Would you mind running over there for me before dinner?"

"No problem, Mom," Zack said. "Can I take your car, though?"

"It's pretty low on gas," his mother said.

"I'll get you some," Zack offered.

Mrs. Morris frowned. "But then you'll have to go all the way to Pulaski Avenue, and you'll be late for dinner. The gas station is right on my way to work, so I can get it tomorrow morning. Why don't you just take the Mustang?"

"Why not," Zack said, sighing.

"Oh, and can you pick me up a few things while you're there?" his mother asked.

"Oh, no!" Zack groaned good-naturedly. "A drugstore list from a female person. I'll be there all night."

"Don't be silly, sweetie. Let's see...I need some of those little cotton balls, and a hot oil-treatment, and jojoba shampoo—"

"Hohoba?" Zack said.

"—oh, and if you see some of that new moisturizer they're advertising on TV..."

Zack clutched his head in horror, and his mother burst out laughing. "Okay, okay. I know I'm impossible. I'll come with you. We can pick up ice cream for dessert."

Mrs. Morris ran for her purse, and Zack grabbed his car keys. Chances were pretty slim that he'd run into Denny Vane. Especially since, thanks to him, Denny Vane now didn't have wheels. Zack sighed. Every once in a while, he'd forget how much bending the truth complicated your life. But better a complicated life than a broken face!

▲   ▼   ▲

The next morning, Zack scanned the walkway to school as Slater expertly maneuvered his '57 Chevy into a parking space. Students were standing around, talking and laughing, spinning out every last second before the bell. There was no sign of Denny Vane lurking in the hall.

As Slater got out of the car, a decrepit Volkswagen bug painted an awful shade of lime green chugged into the space next to his Chevy. The engine switched off with a small explosion. Who was driving such a bomb?

Then, to Zack's surprise, Denny Vane slowly unfolded himself out of the tiny front seat.

"What are *you* looking at?" Denny snarled.

"Me? Nothing," Zack said quickly.

"Hey, Denny," Jessie said. "What happened to your bike?"

"That's what I'd like to know," Denny said, slamming his car door. It popped open again, so he kicked it. The handle fell off, and he put it in his pocket. A group of kids standing near the car snickered. Denny shot them a murderous look, and they quickly scurried on.

"Some piece of sleazy slime trashed it yesterday and drove away," Denny said. "Some people just don't have manners, you know?"

"I agree, absolutely," Jessie said.

Denny scanned the quad ahead. "And, naturally, nobody saw anything. Nada. Even though the chess club was having this meeting, and their window overlooks the parking lot. But the little weasels are too scared to talk. Can you believe it?"

"Mmmm," Slater said. "Hard to believe."

Denny hooked his fingers in his jeans. "I'm going to find a witness if I have to tear apart Bayside High brick by brick. And when I find the guy who creamed my bike, it'll be pasta la vista, baby."

Jessie giggled. "That's *hasta* la vista, Denny. Unless you're going to feed him spaghetti."

Denny scowled. "I'm going to eat the swamp thing for breakfast."

"Sounds yummy," Jessie teased. "Is that a new cereal? Swamp Thing Flakes?"

Zack couldn't believe that Jessie had the nerve to tease Denny Vane. But Denny wasn't a bully when it came to girls. He just ignored Jessie's teasing and adjusted his ponytail self-consciously.

"Uh, catch you later," he mumbled. Then he loped off toward school.

Sweat beaded up on Zack's forehead as he watched Denny walk off, peering at every student suspiciously. He shuddered. Denny was really on the warpath.

▲   ▼   ▲

Across the quad, Kelly saw Zack get out of Slater's car. She waved at him, but he started to talk to Denny Vane and didn't see her. Hugging her books, Kelly smiled to herself. Zack was such a great guy. He was friendly to everybody. Everybody liked him. Even tough guys like Denny Vane who didn't like *anybody* liked Zack.

Of course, there could be occasional drawbacks to having such a popular boyfriend. Take girls. All the girls at Bayside High were crazy about Zack. Even though Kelly knew that Zack loved her, she was in touch with reality. Zack liked girls. He liked to look at them and he liked to flirt with them. Bayside was full of temptations, and a friendly guy like Zack attracted attention wherever he went.

But Kelly trusted him. Things between them were perfect. They'd had some rough patches a while ago, but now, it was smooth sailing. She and Zack hadn't had one teeny problem in weeks. Even yesterday, when she'd thought he'd stood her up, it had all been just a misunderstanding.

Jean-Marie Howell started up the stairs, and she waved at Kelly. Jean-Marie was on the cheerleading team with her, and Kelly really liked her.

"Hiya, Kelly," Jean-Marie said, stopping to

talk to her. She eyed Kelly's pink mini and little white T-shirt. "I don't know how you stay so slim when you eat all that ice cream. Triple peanut fudge goes straight to my hips."

"What do you mean, Jean-Marie?" Kelly asked, laughing. "I don't even *like* triple peanut fudge."

"There's no way Zack could have eaten that whole quart by himself," Jean-Marie said. "I saw him at Mamie's Ice Cream Parlor ordering a quart to go. Then he got into the car with you. I waved, but you didn't see me. At least, I *thought* it was you." Jean-Marie frowned. "It was definitely a girl." Realizing what she'd said, she looked uneasy. Then she looked at Kelly in an interested way. Her nose twitched, as if she'd caught the scent of really good gossip.

Kelly felt as though a ton of bricks had fallen on her head. But she had to cover up. Jean-Marie was one of the worst gossips at Bayside. Kelly tried to laugh. "Oh, right. I got confused because you said I ate ice cream. Can you believe that Zack polished off that entire quart by himself?"

"Oh," Jean-Marie said, looking disappointed. "Well, see you."

Kelly murmured a good-bye, but her eyes were on Zack as he strolled up the walk with Jessie and Slater. He caught sight of her and waved.

Kelly waved back, smiling. "You snake," she said through gritted teeth. Zack had lied to her. His car hadn't broken down yesterday. He'd had another date. He was seeing someone else behind her back!

Chapter 3

▲　▼　▲　▼　▲

When the bell rang for lunch period, Zack was primed for a major pig-out. He'd been too nervous to eat breakfast this morning. As he walked to the cafeteria, he scanned the crowded halls for Kelly. Usually, they met up outside Kelly's English class and walked together. But he hadn't seen much of Kelly this morning. Every time he'd caught up to her, she'd had to run either to speak to a teacher before class or to get a different book from her locker.

The special today was vegetable lasagna and garlic bread. Perfect. Zack grabbed a tray and loaded it up with food and a big glass of milk. Then he went to his regular table, where Screech and Jessie had just sat down with Slater, who was already eating. *Nobody* beat Slater to the cafeteria.

Zack said hello and inhaled the aroma of

rich tomato sauce, garlic, and basil. Even Ms. Meadows, the new cafeteria chef who was totally into health food, couldn't mess up lasagna.

"So what's happening, you guys?" Zack asked as he forked up his first delicious bite. "Is there any late-breaking story I should know about?"

"Mmmpphhh," Slater said, chewing.

Jessie rolled her eyes. "Swallow, you caveman. Then talk."

Slater swallowed. "I heard that Denny Vane figured out who creamed his bike."

Zack choked, and a piece of zucchini shot out of his mouth and into Jessie's glass of milk. She wrinkled her nose. "Whoa, gross."

Zack pushed his milk across the table. "Take mine," he said in a choked voice. "What did you hear, Slater?"

"Ron Noland saw everything," Slater said, breaking off a piece of his garlic bread. "He's in the chess club, and he'd just finished a match and had gone to the window to look out. But he was polishing his glasses at the time, so he didn't see very *clearly*. Just a white blur, he said. And then when he put his glasses back on, he saw something green on the bumper of the car."

"Not much to go on," Jessie said. "There's plenty of white cars at Bayside. Even Zack has a white car."

Zack laughed hollowly. "Right. Not much to go on," he said. Apparently, Jessie had forgotten plastering that GREEN TEENS LOVE TREES bumper sticker on his car.

"Yeah, well, Denny's planning to wrap up the case by this afternoon," Slater said. "He's checking out all the white cars in the parking lot to see if there's red paint from his bike on any of them. The poor guy who did it is going to be in major trouble."

Jessie snitched a piece of garlic bread off Slater's plate. "I don't know why the person doesn't just confess. Denny Vane is all bluff. He's a pussycat."

Slater snatched back his bread. "Yeah, like a big jungle cat. He belongs in a zoo."

"Maybe the person is really scared," Screech said. "It wouldn't be very easy to face Denny Vane. I sure wouldn't want to. But I bet the person's conscience will start bothering him, and he'll confess." He nodded and scooped up a bite of lasagna. "What do you think, Zack?"

"I don't know," Zack said. "I don't know if people are that honest."

"Well, they should be," Screech said.

"Screech, if you ever want to join the real world, let me know," Slater said, his mouth twisting sardonically. "I'll give you a guided tour of reality."

"Thank you, Slater," Screech said, nodding thoughtfully. "I might take you up on that."

A fine film of sweat had broken out on Zack's forehead, and he wiped it discreetly with his napkin. Denny was getting closer. What was he going to do? He couldn't hide a white car with a green bumper sticker forever.

He'd have to soak that bumper sticker off his car tonight, Zack decided. He had a date with Kelly, but he'd tell her he had to study for his history quiz. She was worried about his grade, so she'd understand. His girlfriend was the best. At least *that* part of his life was going just fine.

▲   ▼   ▲

That afternoon, Lisa was checking on the supply of fresh hospital gowns when the light for Room 313 went on.

"Not again," Mary Jo Turner groaned. She was a young nurse who was Lisa's favorite. She turned and looked at Lisa, her bright blue eyes pleading. "Would you check on Mr. Wintergreen for me, Lisa? He probably just wants another pillow or something. He's never satisfied."

Lisa couldn't refuse Mary Jo anything. She covered for Lisa when she was late, or if she had a hot date and wanted to leave a few minutes early.

"Sure," she said, even though it was the last thing in the world she wanted to do.

She pushed open the door to Room 313. Buck Wintergreen was working at a laptop computer, which was balanced on his tray.

"Lucky me," he said sardonically when he saw her. "It's you again."

"What can I do for you, Mr. Wintergreen?" Lisa asked.

"I need you to raise my bed higher. This dang button isn't working properly. What's the matter with this hospital, anyway?"

Maybe we're spending too much on salaries for the board members instead of on equipment, Lisa almost said. But she just went over and pushed the button for the bed to rise. It didn't move.

"I've *done* that already," Buck said. "I'm not an idiot, you know. The hospital nurses have that role taken."

"Crank," Lisa said. Buck looked startled, and she added sweetly, "I'll use the bed crank and do it manually."

He glared at her suspiciously, but Lisa quickly bent down to reach the crank.

Buck quickly put the pitcher of ice water on his night table. "Okay, go ahead. Just be careful!"

Lisa gave the crank a twist, and the bed shot up quickly. Buck banged his head on his computer screen.

"You idiot!" he yelled. "Now look what you've done. As if I'm not in enough pain already! I'm going to get a headache now, thanks to you. How did you get this job, anyway?"

Lisa bit her lip as tears sprang to her eyes. Nobody ever talked to her like that, not even Nurse Moore. Buck Wintergreen deserved to be told off, but she had to keep her mouth shut. One of Nurse Moore's most important rules was to *never talk back to the patient.*

She started to back away. Buck Wintergreen made her so nervous! If he didn't yell and complain so much, maybe she'd be able to concentrate.

"If there's nothing else then, I'll be going," she said, moving backward toward the door.

"Good riddance," Buck said, rubbing his head.

Suddenly, Lisa tripped over an extension cord. She flew backward but was able to steady herself on the windowsill. The cord jerked out of the socket.

"And now look what you've done!" Buck Wintergreen exploded. "You just made me lose a crucial report!"

"I'm really sorry," Lisa said. "But the cord was right in the middle of the fl—"

"I spent all afternoon on it!" he bellowed. He reached for the buzzer to summon the nurse. He held it down with his thumb.

"You know, you really should save your document as you go along," Lisa advised.

"Don't you dare give me advice, young lady!" Buck shouted.

Just then, Nurse Moore rushed in. When she saw Lisa, she closed her eyes for a split second. Then she said in a clipped tone, "Miss Turtle, wait out in the hall for me, please."

"Yes, Nurse Moore." Lisa scurried past her into the hall. There, she heard the murmur of Nurse Moore's soothing voice punctuate Buck's bellows.

But she couldn't make out what either one was saying.

After a few minutes, Nurse Moore barreled out of the room. She crooked her finger at Lisa and led her down the hallway.

"Mr. Wintergreen is very upset," Nurse Moore said, sounding more exasperated than angry. "Lisa, are you *trying* to torture that man?"

"It's just that he keeps yelling at me, and it makes me nervous," Lisa said.

"It's not your job to be nervous," Nurse Moore snapped. "It's your job to be calm. The *patients* are nervous, Lisa. They're scared, and sometimes they're in pain. That's why some of them can be irritable and difficult."

"I know that," Lisa mumbled. She *did* know that. But she couldn't imagine Buck Wintergreen being afraid of anything. He was just plain mean.

"Nurse Moore, can't you transfer me to another ward?" Lisa asked pleadingly. "Mr. Wintergreen wouldn't mind, that's for sure."

Nurse Moore paused. "I'm sorry, Lisa. I can't do that. This is where you're needed. You're just going to have to control your nerves around Mr. Wintergreen."

"But—"

"Lisa," Nurse Moore said, "if I seem to be harder on you than the other candy stripers, it's because sometimes my instinct tells me that you could have a real gift for medicine. If you'd drop

that frivolous pose of yours, maybe you'd discover a
dedicated person underneath."

Lisa didn't know what to say. Nurse Moore
sounded almost human. "Thank you, Nurse Moore,"
she said. "I think."

Nurse Moore frowned. "That doesn't mean
you don't have a long way to go. Starting right now.
Return to your duties, Miss Turtle." She spun
around and marched down the hall, her starched
white back stiff and perfectly straight.

▲   ▼   ▲

That evening, Kelly almost regretted her
coolness to Zack that day. He had seemed so jumpy
and nervous. She knew that he was worried about
his history grade. Maybe Jean-Marie had been
wrong. Maybe it hadn't even been Zack Jean-Marie
had seen. Jean-Marie was too vain to wear her glasses outside of class. She was always jumping up to
cheer when the other team made a goal.

Kelly hadn't been very sympathetic when
Zack had canceled their date to study, and she felt
guilty about it. Zack had seemed really downcast.
Mr. Loomis had told him that he might not gradu-
ate! And she hadn't been sorry for Zack at all. She'd
been too angry.

But didn't he deserve a chance to explain?

Kelly picked up the phone and tentatively

punched out his number. Zack's mother answered the phone.

"Hi, Mrs. Morris. It's Kelly. Can Zack come to the phone?"

"Oh, hi, Kelly," Mrs. Morris said. "Zack isn't here. Actually, I thought he was with you."

"Oh," Kelly said. "He's not."

"Well, let's see. He called upstairs to me about a half hour ago and said he was going out. I heard the garage door, so I guess he took his car. Listen, do you want me to tell him to give you a call when he gets in?"

"No, thanks," Kelly said. "Don't bother. I have a lot of studying to do. I'll just see him in school tomorrow."

She said good-bye and hung up the phone. Give Zack a chance to explain? she fumed. Why bother? That snake would just wiggle and squirm his way out of it. That rat would just lie to her again!

▲   ▼   ▲

Only an hour left to go on her shift. Lisa couldn't wait to get home and slip into a hot bath. She'd pour in a double portion of bath gel for extra bubbles. And she wouldn't come out until she'd soaked every single bit of Wintergreen out of her system.

Mary Jo checked her watch. "Time for the

dinner trays, Lisa." She smiled at her sympathetically. "Last chore and then you can head home. You
look beat."

"I am," Lisa admitted.

"Tell you what. If you finish early, you can
go right home. I'll cover for you with Moore the
Maniac."

"You're a doll," Lisa said gratefully. She
pushed the cart down the hall, distributing the trays
to the various rooms. The patients on this floor were
here for elective surgery, so they weren't too sick.
They were all glad to see the dinner trays.

She hesitated outside of Room 313. But she
only had to see Buck one more time, and then she
could go home. Her next day to work wasn't until
Saturday afternoon, and he was scheduled to be
released on Friday.

Lisa balanced the tray and opened the door.
Buck was reading some kind of report, and he didn't
even look up.

"Dinner," she said brightly.

"After today's lunch, you'll understand if I
don't give a cheer," Buck said dryly. He still didn't
look up.

Lisa slid the tray onto Buck's bed tray.
"You'd better eat it while it's hot," she advised. "If
you think hospital food is bad, you should try *cold*
hospital food."

Buck absentmindedly reached for his fork.
He stuck it in a piece of chicken, then raised it to his

mouth. Suddenly, his face changed, and he threw the fork back on the tray. It clanged against the metal.

Buck seemed to notice her for the first time. "You!" he said, pointing at her. "You're trying to poison me!"

"Me? I didn't cook it! If you knew me, you'd know how ridiculous that idea is," Lisa babbled nervously. "Besides, you didn't even taste it."

Buck pointed to his plate. "I'm allergic to mushrooms. If I ate this dinner, I'd swell up like a balloon."

"Nobody told me," Lisa said.

"Why didn't you try reading my chart?" Buck shouted.

Lisa clasped her shaking hands together. "That's not my job," she said quietly. "The dietician is supposed to—"

"So you just go around poisoning patients?"

"Mr. Wintergreen," Lisa said determinedly, "please calm down. I'll get you another meal."

"Forget it! I'm not eating one morsel of food in this hospital!" Buck yelled. "I'll never make it out of here alive!"

"Mr. Wintergreen, you have to keep your voice down," Lisa said. "There are other patients on this floor. And besides," she muttered to herself, "Nurse Moore will hear you." That was all she needed!

"Nurse Moore is right behind you," Nurse

Moore said. Lisa's heart fell. The woman was every-where! On those crepe-soled white shoes, Lisa never heard her coming.

Buck pointed a shaking finger at Lisa. "Nurse Moore, I want you to fire this incompetent right now!"

That did it. Lisa turned furiously to Buck. "You might be on the board, Mr. Wintergreen, but you don't run this hospital. And you're not the only patient in it. No wonder you get bad service when you bully people like you do. You've got the nurses running scared and neglecting their other patients just to do your bidding! If you really cared about Palisades General, you wouldn't act like such a...a...nincompoop!" Lisa finished, sputtering.

"Miss Turtle!" Nurse Moore exclaimed.

Lisa turned to Nurse Moore. "Don't bother firing me. Because I quit!"

Chapter 4

▲　▼　▲　▼　▲

Avoiding Mary Jo, Lisa grabbed her purse from behind the nurses' station and ran to the elevator. She punched the button for the lobby. She'd never, ever set foot in this hospital again. She must have been crazy to think she'd ever want a medical career!

Lisa dashed through the lobby and pushed through the revolving doors to the parking lot. Her car was only a few lanes away, and she hurried toward it. But as she ran, she heard a high-pitched voice.

"Andy! Andy!" The woman's voice was panicked.

Lisa turned and saw a mother on her knees in front of a small toddler. The little boy's face was pale, and his eyes rolled in fright. Suddenly, Lisa noticed that his lips were blue. He was choking!

Lisa threw down her purse and ran toward them as the mother began to scream.

"He's not breathing!" she wailed. "Andy!"

Lisa didn't hesitate. She pushed the mother aside and picked up the child. She turned him over her knee and hit him hard between the shoulder blades, once, twice, then three times. The third time, a piece of hard candy rocketed out of his mouth and hit the sidewalk. The child began to cough and cry.

"There you go, sweetheart," Lisa murmured, picking him up and patting him. "You'll be just fine in a minute." She gave him to his mother. "He was choking on a piece of candy," she explained. "He's just scared now. He'll be fine."

Tears were streaming down the mother's face. "You saved his life."

Lisa shook her head, smiling. "Anybody could have."

"But you did," the mother said, rocking the child against her. "Thank you. We were just going in to see Andy's grandfather, and I'm sure he'd want to thank you, too."

"Don't mention it," Lisa said, embarrassed. "Well, have a nice afternoon."

"Wait. At least tell me your name," the woman said.

"Lisa Turtle," Lisa said. "I'm—I was a candy striper here."

"I'm Amanda Munroe," the woman said. "My father, Buck Wintergreen, is a patient here. Thank you, Lisa."

Wintergreen! Lisa peered at the woman's bright blue eyes. If Andy was Buck Wintergreen's grandson, that meant that Amanda was his daughter. Immediately, Lisa began to back away. "Bye, now!" she called. She picked up her purse and quickly made her way to her car.

Lisa slid into the driver's seat and fumbled for her keys. Her hands were shaking, so she stopped looking for them and took a deep breath. She still felt a little rattled by the encounter. It wasn't every day she quit her job and saved a little kid's life, all in the space of five minutes!

She definitely needed a moment or two to calm down. Lisa sat, watching visitors walk in and out of the hospital and waiting for her heartbeat to slow down. She felt depressed, and she wasn't sure why.

She'd thought that leaving Palisades General forever would make her happy. She tried to think of the beach days she'd gain, not to mention the additional mall time. But, somehow, even the thought of shopping didn't make her feel better. This must be serious!

If only she didn't feel as though she'd let Nurse Moore down. How come old Moore the Maniac had to turn into a human being all of a sudden? And the thought of telling her parents was a total drag.

But it wasn't just that. A few minutes ago, she'd seen how important her job could be. Now she felt almost sad to be leaving it. She felt so confused!

Suddenly, she saw Amanda Munroe run out of the revolving doors of the hospital, look around the parking lot, and head straight for Lisa's car. What was going on?

"I'm so glad you're still here," Amanda said, panting as she came up. "Dad really wants to talk to you."

"Dad" must be Buck, Lisa thought. "I'm on my way home," she said nervously. Had she done something wrong? Should she have called a doctor? Buck Wintergreen was probably just going to yell at her again.

"Please, Lisa? He really wants to see you."

"Oh. Well. Okay," Lisa said finally. She reluctantly slid out of the car and followed Amanda through the hospital lobby to the elevator.

When they pushed open the door of Room 313, Lisa saw something she hadn't seen before in that room—a smile. Andy sat on the edge of Buck Wintergreen's bed, his little legs swinging. Buck was smiling and ruffling his grandson's blond hair.

He looked up and saw Lisa. His smile didn't even falter. "Here's the heroine," he said. "I appreciate you coming back up, Lisa. I had to thank you for my grandson." His brown eyes twinkled. "And my daughter here tells me I have to apologize for making your life miserable."

"I know how impossible he can be," Amanda said to Lisa. She threw her father a fond glance.

"Oh, he wasn't too bad," Lisa said.

Amanda laughed. "You don't have to be polite, Lisa. He tells me you managed to stand up to him. I approve. It's a good idea to bite back."

"I hate being in the hospital," Buck grumbled. "It gives me the creeps."

"So you have to submit everyone here to your bad mood?" Amanda demanded sternly.

Buck softened when he looked at his daughter. Then he looked guilty. "I couldn't help it. I've never been sick a day in my life. This is highly inconvenient."

Amanda sighed. "You'll be out of here soon, Dad."

"If I live that long," Buck muttered.

"For heaven's sake, it's a hernia operation," Amanda said in exasperation. "Don't be such a baby."

Lisa couldn't help giggling. Slender, fragile-looking Amanda was just as tough as her father.

"Speaking of babies," Buck said, patting Andy's shoulder, "you saved our pride and joy, Lisa. We can never repay that."

"Don't worry about it," Lisa said. "It's my job."

"That doesn't mean we can't *try* to repay you," Buck continued.

Lisa shook her head. "I don't want you to repay me," she said. "Really."

"How about a couple of days of fresh air, sunshine, and relaxation?" Buck queried.

When Lisa looked puzzled, Amanda broke in. "We have a family cabin up in the mountains. It's nothing fancy, believe me. But Dad thought you and your friends might enjoy it. It's just sitting there, empty."

"It should be beautiful up there now," Buck said. "No snow, of course, so you can't ski. But there's hiking and fishing."

"I couldn't," Lisa said. "Really."

Buck looked over the top of his grandson's head. The expression in his dark eyes was sincere. "I would be honored if you would, Lisa. For Andy's sake."

"Please," Amanda said.

Amusement danced in Buck's glittering brown eyes. "That is," he said, "if you could bring yourself to take a favor from a nincompoop."

Lisa giggled. "Well, as one nincompoop to another," she said, "I accept."

▲   ▼   ▲

"Wait a second," Zack said the next day at school. "Let me get this straight. You whack a little kid on the back, and some old guy gives you the keys to his mountain hideaway?"

"That's right," Lisa said.

She could hardly wait to get to school that morning to tell the gang at once. They all stood around her locker, listening incredulously to her story. "Except I didn't just whack him on the back. I saved his life."

"Right," Slater said. "You turn a kid over your knee and a piece of candy falls out."

"You really lucked out, Lisa," Jessie said.

"Really," Zack said. "I always say, if you're going to save a kid's life, it should be a *rich* kid."

"Leave it to Lisa," Slater guffawed. "She must have seen the kid get out of a Mercedes."

Lisa began to get annoyed. It wasn't that she wanted people to think of her as some kind of heroine. But, then again, a little praise and awe wouldn't be so bad.

"If you guys don't watch it, I won't invite you with me," she warned. She jingled the keys in front of their faces. "I'm sure it's a fabulous place. Mary Jo told me that Buck is a zillionaire. Just think. A hot tub *and* a Jacuzzi. A heated indoor pool. Maybe even a steam room."

"That sounds so great," Kelly said.

"A satellite dish so we can get hundreds and hundreds of channels," Lisa elaborated.

"*Now* you're talking," Screech said.

Zack looked at Kelly. She hadn't said much during Lisa's story. As a matter of fact, she looked kind of pale and sad. He slipped his arm around her.

"It sounds pretty romantic," he murmured. "A real getaway."

Kelly slipped out from under his arm and drew closer to Lisa. "How did your parents react to you quitting your job, Lisa?" she asked.

Zack frowned. What was going on?

"Were they super upset?" Jessie asked.

"Oh, they went ballistic," Lisa said, waving her hand in a vague way. But, actually, her parents *hadn't* been that upset. They'd been pretty understanding. They had said that medicine was a tough profession and they understood that it might not be right for Lisa. Somehow, it had made her feel worse.

"Well, at least you don't have to deal with that hospital anymore," Jessie said.

"Not to mention Nurse Moore," Zack said.

"You must be really relieved," Kelly added.

"You said it, girlfriend," Lisa said. "I haven't been this happy since I found a pair of Mario Fanelli suede boots on sale."

"I can't wait to get away," Jessie said. "Let's leave right after school on Friday."

Zack looked at Kelly. She was avoiding his gaze. Maybe she was upset because he kept breaking dates this week. But he was so paranoid about Denny seeing his car that he had to keep canceling.

When he'd spent last night soaking the bumper sticker off his car, he'd noticed deep scratches of telltale red paint. Somehow, he'd have to raise enough cash to bring the car in for bodywork. At least then the car would *really* be out of service. He wouldn't have to lie to Kelly anymore.

This weekend couldn't come at a better time, Zack reflected as the bell rang for homeroom. It was time to get out of town. And it was time to make it all up to Kelly. A romantic weekend would set everything right again. He was sure of it.

▲　▼　▲

After school that day, Zack hung up the phone in disgust. When he joined the others by the stairs, they looked at him glumly.

"My mother said no way," Zack said. "She's not letting me drive for three hours and stay on my own in a remote cabin without supervision. She actually thinks I could get into trouble. Can you believe it?"

"Don't worry about it, Zack," Jessie said. "My mother won't let me go without an adult chaperon, either."

"My mother's words were: 'Over my dead body,'" Lisa said glumly.

"Mine just laughed hysterically," Slater said.

"Gee," Screech said. "Mine told me to have a good time. But then she asked if I'd be home by nine o'clock."

"My mother said there had to be an adult on

the premises, too," Kelly said. "You know the routine. 'It's not that I don't trust you, honey. But...'"

"Those buts will get you every time," Jessie agreed sorrowfully. "Say adios to our beautiful mountain weekend. Good-bye, pine trees."

"Good-bye, romantic crackling fireplace," Zack said.

"Good-bye, long hikes through the woods," Slater said.

"Good-bye, clear mountain lakes," Kelly said.

"Good-bye, hot tub," Lisa said.

Screech cleared his throat. "Good-bye, toasting marshmallows at a romantic crackling fire after a soak in the hot tub while looking at pine trees after going for a long hike to a clear mountain lake," he said quickly, ending up out of breath.

"Oh, well," Zack said philosophically. "I guess this proves it—sometimes, incredible as it may seem, adults *do* come in handy."

"Maybe we could *find* an adult to come with us," Jessie said.

Slater snickered in disbelief. "Think about it this way, momma," he said. "What adult would be crazy enough to agree to hang out with us for an entire weekend in a remote location away from civilization?"

Jessie nodded gloomily. "You're right. We'd have to find a total sap."

Just then, Mr. Belding walked up. "Hey, gang," he said. "What's up?"

Slowly, a grin spread over Zack's face. "Mr. Belding! Well, what do you know. We were just talking about you!"

Chapter 5

▲　▼　▲　▼　▲

Mr. Belding beamed. "You were? How nice."

"We were talking about how hard you work," Zack said. "And how much we appreciate it."

"You *were*?" Mr. Belding asked, surprised. Then he looked suspiciously at Zack. "What do you want?"

"Nothing, Mr. Belding," Zack said. "It's just that we're feeling kind of guilty, you see. We're going on this fabulous weekend getaway, and we were thinking of you stuck here in Palisades."

Zack waited for Mr. Belding to rise to the bait. Spending the weekend with your principal did not exactly make for optimum enjoyment. But it sure beat staying home!

Mr. Belding crossed his arms. "Where are

you kids off to?" he asked in an interested way.

"The mountains," Zack replied. "Lisa has the keys to a fantastic cabin with a hot tub and a heated indoor swimming pool."

"Sounds great, gang," Mr. Belding said. "Mrs. Belding is going to visit her sister in Cleveland, so I get to be a couch potato. There's a really good golf tournament on TV on Saturday. Can't wait."

This wasn't working the way he'd planned, Zack thought nervously. Mr. Belding wasn't jealous at all. "Just think of all that fresh mountain air," he said dreamily. "The peacefulness of the pine forest. The stillness of a clear mountain lake, the cheerfulness of a rushing icy stream—"

"Lakes? Streams?" Mr. Belding perked up. "I haven't fished in ages."

"It's got the best fishing in California," Lisa piped up.

"The best fishing in the *country*," Zack elaborated. "This place is famous. *Angler* magazine did a whole issue on it."

"I never heard of *Angler* magazine," Mr. Belding said thoughtfully.

"You should pick it up sometime," Zack said, even though he'd just made up the magazine. He could always say it had gone out of business. "Anyway, the streams are chock-full of trout and salmon and swordfish—"

"Swordfish is an ocean fish, Zack," Mr. Belding said, frowning.

"You see how incredible this place is?" Zack said.

"So what's the name of this incredible place?" Mr. Belding asked.

"Last Chance, California," Lisa told him.

"Hmmm. Never heard of it."

"It's the best-kept secret in California," Zack assured him.

"Well, have a wonderful time, kids," Mr. Belding said. "I'm just going to—"

"The cabin has three bedrooms," Zack said. "The guys are going to bunk in one, the girls in the other. That leaves the master bedroom free. It wouldn't be fair if the girls or the guys got it."

"Isn't that the bedroom with the adjoining bathroom?" Slater asked.

"With the steam room?" Lisa said.

"You know, I used to be a pretty decent fisherman," Mr. Belding said. "I caught the biggest bass at Willow Lake three years in a row. And I just bought a new lure, too. I keep buying lures, even though Mrs. Belding never wants to go fishing."

Talk about fishing. Zack had a big one on the line now! "How about that," he said. "Hmmm. Maybe we should just flip a coin to see who gets the master bedroom."

"Boy, it would be so nice to get away," Mr.

Belding said meaningfully. "As you pointed out, Zack, a principal's life is rough. Thanks to you kids, I'm completely stressed out."

"Doesn't the master bedroom have its own TV?" Zack asked Lisa.

"Plus, I really get lonely when Mrs. Belding is away," Mr. Belding said, looking at them mournfully.

Zack snapped his fingers. "Hey, wait a second. I just thought of something. Mr. Belding, why don't you come with us? You can sort of keep an eye on things. Make sure we don't get out of hand. Not that we *would*. Is that okay, gang?"

"I guess so," Slater said.

"Sure, why not?" Jessie said.

"We'd love to have you come, Mr. B," Kelly said.

"It would be fun," Lisa said.

"Plus, we need a chaperon," Screech said, but Zack stepped on his foot—hard. "Ow!"

Mr. Belding didn't hear Screech. He was too busy casting an imaginary line into the hallway. "Well, well, what a big surprise. I'd be delighted to come."

"So we'll leave Friday afternoon for Last Chance, California!" Jessie said excitedly.

"I'll bring up the groceries for dinner the first night," Mr. Belding said. "Wait until you taste my tuna noodle casserole. And we'll all go to bed early so we can get up at sunrise for a mountain hike. I'm an expert on mountain flora and fauna."

"Oh, so you know people in Last Chance," Screech said. "Are Flora and Fauna sisters?"

But Mr. Belding was already moving off, muttering to himself about lures and tuna fish.

"Tuna noodle casserole?" Jessie said.

"Getting up at sunrise?" Lisa said with a shudder.

"This is *not* my idea of a wild weekend," Slater said with a sigh.

"I don't know why not," Screech said. "I *love* tuna noodle casserole. And if Flora and Fauna come over, we can have a party!"

▲   ▼   ▲

Friday afternoon, Zack bypassed Denny in his usual position checking out cars in the parking lot. He got into Slater's Chevy, where Jessie was already waiting.

"Next stop, Last Chance," Zack said.

"Bad news, preppy," Slater said. "We can't take my car."

"Why not?" Zack asked.

"I just noticed an oil leak. I don't want to take the risk. Sorry, guy."

"We've got a problem," Jessie admitted. "I can't take my mom's car. And Kelly sure can't take her parents' car. She can't leave the rest of her family stranded."

Slater frowned. "Lisa's parents are both on call at the hospital this weekend, so she can't borrow a car. And if we let Screech drive, we might never make it."

Jessie sighed. "We can't all fit in Mr. Belding's little Toyota. What are we going to do?"

"Are you sure your Mustang isn't fixed yet?" Slater asked Zack.

Zack thought fast. After all, he'd be getting right on the highway and zooming out of Palisades. The chances of Denny spotting him were pretty much nonexistent.

"Don't sweat it, guys," he said. "My car is ready after all. I just called the mechanic to check on it."

"Why don't we just drive to the station now and get it?" Slater suggested. "We'd save time."

"Bad idea," Zack said quickly, thinking fast. "You know how long it takes for those guys to figure out what you owe and get the car. And we still have to pack. That could take hours as far as Lisa is concerned."

"We already limited her to two suitcases," Jessie said.

"Why don't you drive us home the way we planned?" Zack suggested. "While the girls are packing, I can head over to the station and get the car. I'll pick you guys up."

"One problem," Slater said. "Lisa and Screech won't fit in your car. They're going to have to ride with Mr. Belding."

"Screech will think it's a treat," Zack said. "And Lisa is so happy to be going she won't care. So drive on, Slater."

Slater started out of the parking lot. Denny was still at the exit. He was examining each car carefully as it left the lot.

Ahead of them was Alan Zobel in his white Valiant. Denny beckoned, and a quaking Alan pulled over to the curb so that Denny could inspect his bumper. Meanwhile, Denny waved Slater on and gave Zack a friendly wave. Scrawny Alan Zobel nervously tripped as he got out of his car.

Zack sank down in his seat. It was almost enough to give a guy a guilty conscience. Thank goodness Slater was already halfway down the block. In another moment, Zack would have been tempted to confess. Now, *that* was temporary insanity.

▲　▼　▲

Four hours later, Zack followed Mr. Belding's green Toyota down the main street of Last Chance. The light was fading as Mr. Belding pulled into a space in front of a café called Vinnie's Place. Zack pulled in next to him.

Everyone climbed out of the two cars, stretching after the long drive. They looked around the town dubiously. The roof to Vinnie's Place was sagging. There was a forlorn-looking superette and a gas station. There was a five-and-ten and a bait-and-tackle shop. There was a boutique called Dora's with a yellow cotton dress in the window that looked like something Zack's aunt Minnie would have worn to a swap meet back in the early sixties.

"Some resort town," Zack said to Lisa.

"It sure is," Screech said enthusiastically.

"At least there's a bait store," Mr. Belding said.

"I wouldn't eat in Vinnie's Place if you paid me," Jessie said with a shudder.

"I think someone should bring Dora into the nineties," Kelly said, eyeing the yellow dress.

Lisa frowned. "Well, what does the town matter? Once we see the cabin, we'll want to spend all our time there, anyway. Let's head out. I'm dying for a good, long soak in that hot tub."

▲　　▼　　▲

"This can't be it," Lisa said as they stood outside the cabin. "We must have taken a wrong turn."

"This is Skyline Road," Zack said.

"Maybe there's *another* Skyline Road," Lisa said.

"Nope," Slater said. "This is it."

"Well, then, it's the wrong cabin."

"Lisa," Jessie said, "there *is* no other cabin on this part of the road."

"But it can't be it!" Lisa wailed. "This place is gross!"

"It's very...rustic," Kelly said doubtfully.

The old wooden structure needed a good coat of paint. The roof looked like a good rain would cause it to cave in. A dilapidated rocker sat on the porch, its cane seat almost worn through.

"Come on, Lisa, let's go inside," Zack urged. "The interior is probably renovated."

"Right," Lisa said, brightening. She fished the keys out of her purse and led the way up the stairs. She turned the key and pushed open the front door.

The door opened into a short hallway. On one side, they could look into the living room. In the dusk, the room looked gloomy. An old couch was against one wall. Matching armchairs in a faded flowered pattern were in front of a fireplace with a bent poker leaning against it. Rag rugs were scattered on an uneven wooden floor.

They peered across the hall. A rickety-looking table sat in a kitchen that Lisa instantly noted did not contain a dishwasher. Dust motes spun in the dusky air. An old refrigerator hummed noisily.

Slater pushed ahead down the hall and poked his head into the other rooms. "There's only one bathroom," he said.

Lisa swallowed. "With a Jacuzzi?" she asked hopefully.

Slater shook his head. "There's not even a bathtub. Just a stall shower."

"Why would Mr. Wintergreen tell you that there was a Jacuzzi if there wasn't?" Kelly wondered as they trooped into the living room.

"Did this guy have it in for you after all?" Slater said, swiping at the faded curtains. Dust puffed out from between the folds, and he sneezed.

Lisa thought for a moment. Buck had never really mentioned a Jacuzzi, she recalled. "I guess I kind of assumed it," she admitted shamefacedly.

The gang looked at her accusingly. "But you should have seen the rock on Amanda's finger!" she defended herself. "I can't see someone with that many carats putting up with no Jacuzzi."

"Did Amanda say that she spent weekends here?" Jessie asked, narrowing her eyes suspiciously.

"Well, no," Lisa said in a small voice. "I guess I kind of assumed it."

"What about the heated indoor pool?" Zack asked her.

"I guess I kind of assumed it," Lisa admitted, her voice getting even fainter.

"And the hot tub?" Slater asked.

"I guess I kind of, you know, assumed it," Lisa said, her voice a whisper.

"I'd like to kind of assume you straight into the lake," Slater grumbled.

Screech returned to the living room from the back of the house. "Guess what? There's no TV." He frowned. "I guess that means that there's no satellite dish."

"No TV? How will we survive?" Lisa wailed.

Mr. Belding rubbed his hands together. "Now, kids, that's enough of this doom and gloom. This place will suit us just fine. Slater, you and Jessie bring the bags in. Lisa, you can start making the beds. Screech, you can help me with the tuna casserole. I brought everything we'll need. Zack, why don't you and Kelly get a fire going? Lisa said there's a cord of wood stacked in the barn. Let's warm up the atmosphere."

"Sounds like a great idea to me," Zack said, giving Kelly a meaningful glance. But Kelly just looked out the window.

Zack frowned. Come to think of it, Kelly had sat against the door all the way up there. And she hadn't talked much to him, just to Slater and Jessie. And when Jessie had said how great it was that Zack's car had been fixed, Kelly had just made a sour face. What had happened to his cheerful, happy girlfriend? Had an alien taken over Kelly's body? Or was he in more trouble than he thought?

He and Kelly had to talk. Tonight would be hard, with everyone here. But they were in a beautiful, remote spot, Zack consoled himself. There would be plenty of opportunities for them to be alone.

Chapter 6

▲ ▼ ▲ ▼ ▲

"I'm really sorry, girls," Lisa said the next morning as they cruised the aisles at the superette in town. "I feel like this is all my fault. Instead of soaking in a hot tub, we're buying toilet tissue and Mr. Belding's favorite granola." She sighed. "We might as well have stayed home in Palisades."

"It's okay, Lisa," Kelly said. "The cabin isn't that bad. It looked better this morning."

"And there's a pretty view of the lake," Jessie said soothingly. "I think we're going to have a great time."

"And wouldn't you rather be buying Mr. Belding's granola than his bait?" Kelly said, wrinkling her nose. "The boys have to pick out worms."

Lisa giggled. "Thank heaven for small favors."

"Small, wiggly favors," Kelly added, laughing.

Jessie consulted the list. "Mr. Belding is promising us fresh fish tonight, so all we need is some rice and a vegetable. Unless you want to have some of that leftover tuna casserole."

Lisa clutched her stomach. "Please. It gave me nightmares."

Kelly grinned. "I gave most of mine to Screech when Mr. Belding wasn't looking. Listen, you guys, you get the granola, and I'll go check out the produce department. Hopefully, they'll have something green. I'll meet you at the checkout."

Kelly headed to the produce section and looked over the vegetables. The broccoli didn't look too bad, but Zack hated broccoli. Suddenly, Kelly smiled. She picked up three large heads of it.

She couldn't believe that rat. She knew him well enough to know that Zack had been feeling guilty about his treachery all week. But the clear mountain air seemed to have blown away his conscience. He was acting like he hadn't done anything wrong!

Kelly had been especially angry at him yesterday, when he'd gone on and on about how great it was to get his car back. What a liar! On Thursday, she had gone over to the Morris house. She'd just had to satisfy her curiosity. She'd peeked in the garage window and seen Zack's Mustang. That was all the proof she'd needed. Zack had been lying to

her about the car so that he could ride around with
that bimbo Jean-Marie had seen him with.

Kelly was going to confront him, of course.
But before that, she was going to torture him. She
was going to make her famous stir-fried broccoli and
make him eat every single bite.

Smiling to herself, Kelly juggled the broccoli as she headed toward the checkout. She almost
bumped into Lisa and Jessie, who had stopped in
the middle of the aisle.

"Hey, you guys, get the lead out," Kelly
said. "I want to go for a hike before lunch and see
some wildlife."

"Shhhh," Lisa said. She put a finger to her
lips, her brown eyes twinkling. "The wildlife is right
here." She pointed toward the checkout.

Puzzled, Kelly followed Lisa's pointing finger. Three guys stood at the checkout, leafing
through a magazine. They were wearing bicycle
shorts, and their bicycle hats were on backward.
They looked up and saw the girls staring, and big
smiles spread over their faces.

"*Buon giorno!*" they all called, waving.

"Frenchmen!" Lisa trilled.

Jessie poked her. "They're Italian, Miss
Linguist."

"Even better," Lisa said, undaunted. "Aren't
they adorable? Things are looking up."

Kelly stood there, hugging her broccoli. The
tallest of the guys had a dimple in one cheek and a

lopsided smile. His eyes were dark and mysterious. He smiled straight at her, and she felt her knees buckle. Her legs felt like overcooked spaghetti. But instead of falling down, she smiled back.

Lisa was right. Things were definitely looking up.

"Come on," Lisa hissed. "Before they go away."

But the Italians were in no hurry. They stood, waiting and smiling, until the girls walked up.

"*Come sta?*" the one with the curly hair said.

"I think that means how are you doing," Jessie told Lisa and Kelly.

"Very good," the handsome one who had smiled at Kelly said. "That is my friend Eugenio. And this is Antonio," he said, pointing to the muscular guy next to him. Then he looked at Kelly. "I am Francesco."

"So romantic!" Lisa breathed.

"I'm Jessie," Jessie said. "This is Lisa and Kelly."

Francesco took Kelly's hand. "Kelly," he murmured. "I am so pleased to meet you."

Eugenio, the curly headed one, beamed at Lisa. She smiled back. "*Buon giorno,*" she tried.

Eugenio's smile grew even wider. He answered her in a flood of Italian.

Lisa held up her hand, laughing. "I don't speak Italian," she told Eugenio.

"It is all right," Eugenio said in his romantic Italian accent. "It does not matter. When a woman is as beautiful as the sun, words are unnecessary."

"Wow," Lisa said. "I love Italy!"

"Why are you guys in Last Chance, California?" Jessie asked curiously. "You're pretty far from home."

"We are training for the Olympics," Francesco answered. "We are on the Italian bicycling team."

"That is so cool," Lisa said.

"We are training on the mountain roads," Antonio explained. "Our coach is very strict. This is our first day off in weeks. And already, we have made good friends." He smiled at Jessie.

"Well," Kelly said, pointing to her broccoli, "we'd better pay. We're holding up the line." Actually, there wasn't anybody behind them. But Francesco was too handsome and was looking at her with too much interest. She felt herself blushing.

Francesco drew near her as she put the broccoli on the checkout lane. "You will make *broccoli all'aglio* tonight?" he asked.

Kelly shook her head. "I'm just going to sauté it with a little garlic and olive oil."

"That's what I said!" Francesco said, laughing. "A little olive oil, a little garlic, a little crushed hot red pepper—" He kissed the tips of his fingers. "Delicious!"

"Crushed pepper," Kelly said. "I'll try it."

Eugenio took the bag of groceries from the checker before Lisa could reach for it. "I'll carry this," he said. "A woman as delicate as you shouldn't have to carry her own bags. I know you American women are very independent, but I am Italian. I believe in pampering a woman, at least until I get married. It's the Italian way."

"I *knew* there was a reason I loved spaghetti!" Lisa said happily.

As they walked out into the brilliant sunshine, Zack, Slater, and Screech were waiting for them. None of the guys looked crazy about the fact that the girls had met three cute guys in the grocery store.

"Those are our friends," Kelly explained to Francesco, pointing toward the guys.

He smiled. "I would like to meet them," he said. "I like American students. You are all so friendly."

I wouldn't be too sure about that, Kelly thought. But she introduced Antonio, Francesco, and Eugenio to the guys and explained why the Italians were in Last Chance. As soon as the guys heard that they were training for the Olympics, they greeted the Italians with a flood of questions.

Soon all the guys were talking together as though they'd known each other for a million years. Kelly, Lisa, and Jessie loaded the groceries into the trunk of Zack's Mustang. Jessie slammed the trunk shut with a groan.

"We should have known," she said. "When it comes to guys, sports are the international language."

When they returned to the group at the front of the car, Francesco said, "I have an idea. Why do you not all come bicycling with us this afternoon after lunch? It is only a short trip to Lake Sequoia."

Zack opened his mouth to refuse. He wanted to spend time alone with Kelly, not share her with three handsome Italians. But Slater was already talking.

"Fantastic!" Slater said. "I'm dying for some exercise."

"Wait a second," Jessie said. "We don't have bicycles."

"That's no problem," Antonio said. "We have extra bicycles."

"Enough for all of us?" Lisa asked.

"But of course. We have extra for our team, and the place where we are staying also has bicycles," Antonio answered. "We can leave ours here and go and get the others."

"It is a piece of cake, as you would say," Francesco said, his eyes warming when his gaze drifted to Kelly.

Eugenio moved closer to Lisa. "Lisa," he murmured. "We will ride together, no?"

Lisa nodded happily. "We will ride together, yes," she said.

Suddenly, a girl walked rapidly toward them. Her curly black hair waved around her thin, pretty face. Her dark eyes flashed when she saw Eugenio talking to Lisa.

"Eugenio!" she said. Then she burst forth in angry Italian. Eugenio answered back sharply. Obviously, they were having an argument. And when the girl pointed to Lisa, she began to get an idea why.

"That's our coach's daughter, Angelica," Francesco told Lisa in a low voice. "She and Eugenio used to go together. She broke up with him, and now she wants him back. He's not interested anymore."

"Angelica," Francesco said in a loud tone, "we have invited these kind Americans to ride with us to Lake Sequoia today. Do you want to come?"

Angelica didn't look too happy about the prospect. She tossed her head and looked angrily at Eugenio. "I will come," she said.

"Sheesh," Lisa said under her breath to Jessie. "Don't do us any favors."

"If I were you, I'd watch out," Jessie said to Lisa in a low tone. "I wouldn't want to tangle with Angelica."

"But if I get to tangle with Eugenio, it might be worth it," Lisa said, shooting him a soft smile. He smiled back, and she sighed. "And to think I used to love Italy for its shoes!"

▲ ▼ ▲

After saying good-bye to the Italians and agreeing to meet back at the superette parking lot in an hour, the gang split up. The girls went to the drugstore. Slater headed off in search of takeout food at Vinnie's because he was nervous about what Mr. Belding was going to fix for lunch. Screech wandered back to the bait-and-tackle store to say good-bye to the worms.

Zack hoisted himself on the back of his car and tilted his face to catch some rays. He wasn't too upset about the afternoon plans. He would go for a hike alone with Kelly at the lake.

The weekend was turning out pretty well, he thought. The cabin looked better in daylight. The Italians seemed like nice guys. Kelly was more cheerful today. And Mr. Belding's tuna casserole was turning into a faint memory.

Zack heard the chug, chug of a car engine. It sounded familiar, as though he'd heard it once in a dream. Or was it a nightmare? An instinctive chill ran up his spine. Zack opened his eyes.

It *was* a nightmare. It had to be. Because he couldn't be seeing what he was seeing. He couldn't be seeing a decrepit lime green Volkswagen bug chugging down Main Street. And he couldn't be seeing Denny Vane at the wheel. Zack pinched himself, but all he got was a sore arm. The vision didn't go away.

There was only one explanation, Zack thought wildly. Denny Vane had finally figured out who'd trashed his bike. And he'd tracked him down!

Chapter 7

▲ ▼ ▲ ▼ ▲

Zack gazed around in panic. Where could he hide? Main Street was wide and empty. And even if Zack could duck into a store and avoid Denny, his car was still blindingly visible.

Just as Zack wondered if he had time to run to Bud's Paint Store and buy a tarp to throw over the Mustang, he saw that Denny had speeded up and was heading straight toward him.

Zack sat frozen as Denny parked the VW bug and loped toward him. Denny stuck out like a sore thumb in tiny little Last Chance. With his ponytail and in his black leather motorcycle jacket, he could have been a visitor from Mars.

Funny, he didn't *look* angry, Zack thought nervously. As a matter of fact, he looked kind of happy to see Zack. He was probably looking forward to breaking his face, Zack decided.

"Whoa," Denny said as he came up. "What do you know. It's a small world, after all. Hey, don't you love that ride in Disneyland? You sit in those little boats going past all those little dolls singing their little hearts out—I love that stuff."

Zack blinked at him, confused. He didn't know what he was more surprised at—Denny's friendly tone or the fact that the biker had been to Disneyland...and actually liked it.

"I liked the Matterhorn," Zack said, dazed. "Those little dolls drove me nuts."

Denny blushed and looked away. "Well, yeah, right, me, too. It's a Small World is for wimps. I meant that it was my *brother's* favorite ride."

"Denny, what are you doing here?" Zack asked. "Not that it's not great to see you," he added quickly.

Denny waved a hand at the street. "My uncle Vinnie needs some help with his place. I'm digging a cesspool."

"That sounds like fun," Zack said enthusiastically. He moved his foot so that it covered the scratch of red paint on his bumper.

"Not really," Denny said, shrugging. "But I get to eat for free."

"So your uncle is Vinnie of Vinnie's Place?" Zack asked.

"Yeah." Denny leaned against the streak of red paint on the left side of the car. "Actually, I don't even mind the work. I had to get out of Palisades. This revenge thing is knocking me out."

"Sorry to hear that," Zack gulped.

"Cross-referencing all those names of guys to the cars they drive...whew. And all those plans for major pulverizing...whoa. Deciding what to *do* to the guy...wow. It's exhausting, man. It's worse than that part-time job I had at Burger World. But at least I don't have to wear a hairnet."

"Well, I'm glad you get to have a little vacation," Zack said.

"You said it," Denny agreed. "Nobody realizes how tiring it is to be a bad dude."

"Hey, wasn't that your uncle Vinnie waving at you down the street?" Zack hinted.

Denny sighed and pushed off the car. "Probably. He's a slave-driving dude. Catch you later, Zack." He loped away and didn't look back.

As soon as Denny was out of sight, Zack slid off the car and headed down the street to round up the gang. He had to get the Mustang safely back to the cabin. He knew one thing—he had to hide it for the rest of the weekend. Because if he wasn't careful, he'd wind up spending his wild weekend in the hospital.

▲   ▼   ▲

Back at the cabin, the gang finished Mr. Belding's liverwurst-and-cream-cheese sandwiches.

"Good lunch, huh?" Mr. Belding said.

"Great," everyone said weakly.

"Tomorrow, *we'll* make lunch," Slater said quickly. "We insist."

The girls ran to change into biking clothes, and Mr. Belding picked up his fishing rod. "Well, men, I'm going to head out to catch our supper."

"Didn't you say that this morning after breakfast, Mr. Belding?" Zack pointed out.

Mr. Belding looked sheepish. "They weren't biting this morning. I have a feeling mountain fish are afternoon feeders."

"Don't worry, Mr. Belding," Screech assured him. "We'll still have a fish supper. There's plenty of tuna noodle casserole left."

Slater looked panicked. "You'd better get out to the lake, Mr. B. I wouldn't want those fish to get away."

Mr. Belding headed out, and Slater and Screech went to put shorts on. Zack headed out to the car. He opened the barn door and pulled the Mustang in. Then he went back inside the house. His friends were adjusting backpacks and filling their water bottles.

Zack paused in the doorway to the living room and gave a theatrical groan. "You're not going to believe this," he announced.

"You're probably right," Kelly muttered.

"The car is out of commission again. The mechanic warned me that this might happen."

"What's the problem?" Slater asked.

"It's a little thingamajig," Zack said. "A little part that I need replaced. I forget the name of it. I'll remember when I go to the auto supply store. The mechanic warned me that this might happen, but I just didn't want to spend the extra money."

"Let me have a look at it," Slater offered.

"No," Zack blurted. Slater was an expert mechanic, and he'd know right away that there was absolutely nothing wrong with the car. "I mean," he said quickly, "it won't do any good. I know exactly what the problem is. I'll stop by the gas station later and pick up the part. I can fix it tomorrow morning. We can still get home, don't worry."

"But what about now?" Lisa said. "We're supposed to meet Eugen—I mean, the Italians in fifteen minutes."

"We can borrow Mr. Belding's car," Zack said. "I'm sure he won't mind. I'll run down to the lake and ask him. We'll be on our way in five minutes."

"Good," Lisa said in relief. "I wouldn't want to disappoint Eugen—I mean, the Italians."

"Me, either," Kelly said. "Francesco was really looking forward to seeing all of us."

Somehow, Zack didn't like the way she said it. And he didn't like the fact that she was blushing, either.

Then she shot him a suspicious look. "Funny how your car broke down *again*, Zack. I mean, it just got back from the mechanic's."

"Yeah," Zack agreed. "That's pretty unbe-lievable."

"That's *really* unbelievable."

"Hey," Screech said, "that's one of my favorite shows. 'That's Really Unbelievable.' If only we had a TV!"

▲ ▼ ▲

Everyone squeezed into Mr. Belding's Toyota, and fifteen minutes later, they pulled up in town. Francesco, Eugenio, Antonio, and Angelica were already waiting with extra bicycles.

"Here you go," Francesco said, leading Kelly to a shiny new mountain bike.

"Here, Jessie, this green bike is for you," Antonio said. "It matches your eyes."

Eugenio wheeled a bright yellow bicycle to Lisa. "I picked this one especially for you," he said softly. He held it steady for her as she mounted it.

Angelica muttered something in Italian, but Lisa ignored it. It was easy since Eugenio was so cute. "Yellow is my favorite color," she told him. Behind her, she heard Angelica stamp her foot, but Eugenio didn't even blink.

"And we got some bicycles from the resort storage room for you guys," Francesco told Zack. "Here they are."

Zack and Slater exchanged glances. Before

them were three old bicycles with peeling paint and only three gears. Zack rolled one out experimentally. It was the sorriest-looking vehicle he'd ever seen outside of Denny's VW bug.

"Are they okay?" Francesco asked anxiously. "They were the best we could find."

Antonio and Eugenio looked at the guys worriedly.

"Okay?" Eugenio asked, concerned.

"They're just fine," Zack assured him. The poor guys looked so anxious to please. He didn't want to be responsible for the breakdown of Italian-American relations.

"Just fine," Slater said.

"It looks just like my bike at home," Screech said.

"Who cares, anyway," Zack said to Slater as they all got on their bikes and began to pedal out of Last Chance. "It's a gorgeous day, and they said it wasn't a hard ride."

"Maybe not for *them*," Slater said, as he struggled to change gears.

Zack pedaled faster to catch up to Kelly. He was just able to keep even with her back wheel. "This is great, isn't it?" he said over the whine of their wheels.

Kelly must not have heard him, for she suddenly started to pump harder and surged forward. She caught up with Francesco, who was in the lead.

Zack tried to pedal faster, but now they

were on a hill. The Italians and the girls shifted gears and took the hill easily. Zack began to pant as the incline grew steeper.

Behind him, he heard Slater grunt. When he looked over his shoulder, he saw that Screech had given up and was walking his bike. When Zack and Slater finally reached the top of the hill, the Italians and the girls were just going out of sight behind a curve. The two boys stopped to wait for Screech.

"Wow," Screech said when he reached them. "It's lucky that we know the way. At least Francesco and Antonio and Eugenio can entertain the girls. It's probably going to take us twice as long to get to the lake."

"And by the time we get there, it will be time to turn around and come back again," Zack said. "We won't get to spend any time with the girls."

"Exactly, preppy." Slater wiped his forehead with the sleeve of his shirt. He squinted at the empty road ahead of them. "Does anyone," he asked, "know the Italian word for *chump*?"

▲   ▼   ▲

Kelly hopped off her bicycle and peered behind her. "I don't see them," she said to Francesco. "Do you think they could have gotten lost?"

"Impossible," Francesco said soothingly. "It is a straight ride here, and you can't miss the lake. You see it from the road. Come," he said, taking her hand. "You must have a closer view. It's a beautiful sight."

Kelly allowed herself to be pulled along through the trees. They passed through a small clearing and reached the edge of the lake. It *was* incredibly beautiful. The water was a deep, sparkling blue. The scent of pine freshened the air. Tall, green mountains with snowy peaks rose up around them.

"It's beautiful," Kelly said in a hushed voice. "I've never seen anything so spectacular."

"I knew you would love it." Francesco looked at her. "I could tell from the moment I met you that you were a woman who appreciates beauty. You are touched in the soul by it, I think."

Kelly smiled shyly. Francesco said such romantic things. She had a prick of conscience about Zack. But why shouldn't she enjoy spending time with Francesco? Zack had lied to her. He didn't deserve her trust.

Ahead of them, they saw Lisa and Eugenio heading toward a dock near a ranger station. Angelica was right behind them.

"You can rent rowboats and canoes there," Francesco said, pointing. "Would you like to do that? It is very peaceful in the middle of the lake."

Kelly gave a quick glance behind her. She really should wait for Zack and the others.

"Ah, you are worried about your friends," Francesco said, nodding. "But I will keep a sharp eye out for them. As soon as they arrive, we will row in. Okay?"

Kelly nodded. "Okay."

▲   ▼   ▲

Zack, Slater, and Screech rode their bicycles down the path and collapsed in a grassy clearing. Ahead of them, the lake sparkled in the sunshine. There was no one in sight.

"Are we sure this is the right lake?" Slater asked.

"If it isn't, I don't care," Zack said with a groan. He flopped onto his back. "I can't move a muscle."

Suddenly, they heard a splash out on the lake and then a shriek of girlish laughter. Slater sat up and squinted.

"Are you sure you don't want to move, preppy?" he asked. "Because it looks like a certain Italian is moving in on your girl."

Zack sat up and looked across the lake. Kelly and Francesco were in a rowboat. They were sitting very close together on the same seat, each with an oar. As Zack watched, Francesco slid even closer.

He caught movement farther down the trail around the lake, and a flash of wavy brown hair. Jessie and Antonio were walking together. Their heads were close, and they were talking intently.

"I'd watch out if I were you, too," he said to Slater, pointing to Jessie with his chin.

"Where's Lisa?" Screech asked, looking around. "I can't see her."

"I suggest you look for Eugenio," Slater said.

Just then, a canoe eased into sight around the trees. Eugenio and Lisa were paddling gently toward the dock where Angelica sat, waiting for them.

"Eugenio," Lisa said, her voice carrying across the water, "there was a big rock near the dock. We should be careful." She twisted behind her, the canoe rocking gently. "Can you see it, Angelica?" she called.

Angelica nodded. "Don't worry. Just come straight in from where you are."

Lisa dipped her paddle in again and gave a strong stroke. Eugenio did it at the same time, and the canoe shot forward. Suddenly, the bottom scraped over something, and the canoe began to tip.

"Eugenio!" Angelica called. "Stand up!"

"No!" Lisa said. "Don't stand, Eugenio! Don't—"

But Eugenio was already rising, and the

canoe tipped over completely. Lisa and Eugenio disappeared. Screech, Slater, and Zack all sprang to their feet. Kelly and Francesco started to frantically row toward the dock, and Jessie and Antonio began to run from the path. But by the time they all reached the dock, Lisa and Eugenio had surfaced and were swimming the few strokes to safety. Lisa was laughing, but Eugenio was looking angrily at Angelica.

Jessie and Antonio ran back to the ranger station for blankets while Zack and Slater helped Lisa onto the dock. Eugenio pulled himself up and stood there, dripping wet and furious. He began to yell at Angelica in Italian. Francesco tried to referee. It appeared that Angelica was protesting her innocence and that Eugenio wasn't buying it.

"Come on, Lisa," Screech said. "You'd better come to the ranger station to get warm. You're shivering."

Lisa followed Screech, and Slater wandered after Jessie and Antonio. Zack found himself alone with Kelly for the first time that weekend.

"Lisa's playing with fire," he observed. "Angelica is really jealous."

"I think Lisa can handle it," Kelly said.

"Maybe you should warn her to take it easy. And maybe you should, too."

Kelly turned to face him. "What is that supposed to mean?"

"I saw you out on the lake with Francesco."

"So?" Kelly asked stonily.

"So, you're my girlfriend, Kelly," Zack said, exasperated. "I don't like to see you with another guy. Sue me."

Kelly raised an eyebrow. "I didn't know I wasn't allowed to go for a boat ride with somebody."

"Kelly, what's wrong?" Zack asked. "Why are you treating me this way? It's not like you."

Kelly's silky hair flew as she jerked her head back to look at the lake. "Maybe I'm tired of being a sap. Maybe this is the new me."

"A sap?" Zack asked, puzzled. "Look, I'm sorry if it seemed like I was neglecting you last week. But you know I had important stuff happening."

"Yes," Kelly said. "I know that, all right."

"If you're trying to make me jealous, it's working," Zack said. "I thought we were going steady."

"So did I," Kelly said. "But, obviously, it was a delusion."

"What are you talking about?" Zack asked.

"Kelly!" Francesco called from the dock. "Come here and see the pretty fish."

"Coming!" Kelly called.

Zack put a hand on her arm. "Kelly, wait a second. I think you owe me an explanation."

"I owe...," Kelly said in a choked voice. She shook off his hand angrily. "You have nerve, Zack Morris!"

"Sure," Zack said, trying to joke. "Isn't that what you love about me?"

But Kelly didn't smile. She just stared at him for a moment, fury blazing in her blue eyes. Then she turned on her heels and stalked away, straight to Francesco's side.

Chapter 8

▲ ▽ ▲ ▽ ▲

"Remind me never to eat pizza again," Zack said later as he biked back to Last Chance with Slater and Screech. Luckily, the ride back to town was easier, since it was mostly downhill.

"This guy Antonio's father is head of some environmental group in Italy," Slater said. "Of course, Jessie is thrilled to hear all about saving the Alps. Give that girl a cause and she's yours."

"I don't even think Francesco is that handsome," Zack said.

"I don't know what Lisa sees in Eugenio," Screech puffed. "What does that guy have that I don't have besides an accent?"

"Try looks, charm, and muscles," Slater said.

"Ah-ha! But does he have hamsters?" Screech crowed triumphantly.

"Well, at least we have one consolation," Slater said. "We'll only be chumps once. We don't have to see these guys again."

Thanks to the downhill journey, they got to Last Chance only fifteen minutes behind the rest of the group. As they coasted to a stop, the girls turned to them excitedly.

"Francesco just had the greatest idea," Lisa said. "He invited us to a picnic tomorrow!"

The guys exchanged glances. "Sounds great," Slater said in a flat voice.

"He knows the perfect spot," Kelly said. "It's only about an hour by bike."

"There's a gorgeous meadow for our picnic," Jessie explained. "It overlooks the valley. You can see for miles. Antonio says that Icebound Peak is even as beautiful as places in Italy."

"Icebound *Peak*?" Slater asked.

Zack, Slater, and Screech gave their bicycles dubious looks. The last thing the boys wanted to do was toil up a mountain on them.

"It is not too many kilometers," Francesco assured them. "And not too much uphill. I know the best way to go. We take a back road that climbs very gradually."

Antonio frowned. "I don't know, Francesco. Maybe even the easy road would be too much for Zack, Slater, and Screech. They are not used to bicycling in the mountains."

"You are right, my friend. Perhaps their legs

could not take the ride," Francesco said, nodding unhappily.

Eugenio looked sorrowfully at them, his big, liquid brown eyes concerned. "So sorry," he said. The three Italians sighed.

Zack wanted to groan. The Italians didn't fool him one bit. They *wanted* Zack and the others to back out. But their honor—not to mention their girlfriends—was at stake.

"Actually, it sounds like a lot of fun," Zack said. "Doesn't it, Slater?"

"Actually—" Slater started.

Zack stepped on his foot and shifted his eyes to Antonio, who was staring soulfully at Jessie. "*Doesn't* it?"

"Absolutely," Slater growled.

"Good. So we all will go," Francesco said approvingly. But Zack could see a tiny shadow of disappointment in his eyes. That Italian lover was dying to get Kelly alone tomorrow! There was no way Zack would let that happen. Even if he had a heart attack pumping that wreck of a bicycle up a mountain, he'd get there.

Then Zack saw Denny Vane coming out of Vinnie's Place. Just when Zack thought he had enough problems!

Zack tried to pretend he didn't see him, but Denny called out his name and hurried toward him.

"Hey, guys," he greeted them.

"Hi, Denny," Zack said. "These are our new

friends—Antonio, Francesco, Eugenio, and Angelica. This is Denny, guys. He goes to our school."

"Hey," Denny said. "You guys are foreigners, right?"

"We're from Italy," Francesco said.

"Cool," Denny said.

"Actually, it's a pretty warm country," Screech said.

"Hey, Zack, I just had to tell you," Denny said. "I have incredible news."

"What's that?" Zack asked politely. Since when had he become Denny's confidant?

"My uncle saw the car that hit my bike right here in Last Chance! Isn't that totally weird?"

Zack felt like all the blood had left his head. "What?" he exclaimed.

"Here?" Slater said.

"That *is* weird," Jessie said.

"How do you know?" Zack asked.

"Well, first of all, it was white. But here's the clincher. Uncle Vinnie painted the bike for me last summer. He knows the shade of red exactly. It was scratched into the side of the car. Uncle Vinnie is positive."

"That's incredible," Zack gulped.

Denny shrugged. "People from here sometimes drive to Palisades for the beach. Maybe some kid drove down and knows someone at school."

"That's a good deduction," Zack said.

"So listen, you guys," Denny said. "I want you to do me a favor. Keep your eye out for the car, all right? I really want to nail this guy. Like, to the wall."

"You bet," Zack promised.

"We'll watch out for it," Lisa promised.

"We train all over around here," Antonio said. "We'll keep our eyes open."

"Thanks. I really appreciate it. Listen, you guys, I have to get back to work. See you."

Denny waved and walked off, his head swiveling as he looked around for the car.

Zack couldn't believe it. Not only was Denny looking for him now, but everybody else was looking for him, too. Even *he* was looking for him! This was the biggest mess he'd gotten himself into yet.

▲   ▼   ▲

Zack didn't think things could get any worse, but they did. Mr. Belding hadn't caught a thing that day, not even a tiny little trout. For dinner, they all got a couple of spoonfuls of the leftover tuna casserole and a huge pile of broccoli. Everyone else thought the Italian-style broccoli was delicious. Since Kelly had made the dish, Zack tried manfully to choke down his least favorite vegetable. But then when he heard it was Francesco's recipe, he lost his appetite.

Worst of all, Kelly barely looked at him. She didn't even give him a chance to apologize. Zack knew that he'd blown it earlier. Girls hated it when you came on strong like that. And he shouldn't have tried to joke when Kelly was so upset.

After dinner, the girls found an Italian guidebook on the living room bookshelves, and they spent the night memorizing phrases to try out on the Italian boys the next day. Slater, Screech, and Zack played cards, wincing every time they heard another burst of laughter from the other corner of the room.

"How about this?" Jessie said. "*Antonio, ancora del cervella, per favore.*"

Kelly giggled as she peeked into the book. "I think you just asked Antonio to serve you more brains, Jessie."

"She could use some more brains," Slater grumbled under his breath. "Anyone who'd be interested in that spaghetti head is an idiot."

Finally, even the girls got tired and said *buona notte* to the guys. Everyone headed off to their own rooms, where Zack, Slater, and Screech could hear the girls giggling. Even the giggling sounded Italian.

Slater fell onto his bed with a crash. "This has got to stop," he muttered. "*Finito.*"

Zack eased off his shoes and sighed. "I'm not looking forward to that ride tomorrow."

"Me, either," Screech said, rubbing his bony calves. "I don't know if I can make it."

"We *have* to make it," Slater said in a fierce

tone. "The honor of the American male is at stake. Those guys can't make chumps out of us again."

"But what are we going to do?" Screech asked. "We can't go out and buy decent bikes tomorrow. And we can't let them go without us."

Zack thought a minute. Then he hit his head with his palm. "We're being so stupid!" he said, sitting up. "Why are we letting those guys set the ground rules?"

"What's cooking in that brain of yours, preppy?" Slater asked, interested. "Whatever it is, I hope it's not tuna casserole."

"Why *should* we have to ride those bikes?" Zack demanded. "Because they told us to? Why don't we just drive Mr. Belding's car to the mountain and *say* we rode the bikes? We'll get there ahead of them and hide the car."

"But what if they see us on the way?" Screech asked.

Zack shrugged. "We'll just make sure they don't. Francesco picked an easy route to get up the side of the mountain, right? It winds all over the place. We'll go up the straight road."

"Wait a second," Slater said. "We have the bikes here. We're supposed to ride down to Last Chance with the girls to meet the Italians. If we send the girls down first, they'll be suspicious."

"We're not going to do that," Zack explained. "We're going to ride to Last Chance and take off with the group. But as soon as they lose us on the first hill, one of us can ride back here and pick up Mr. B's car. Then the driver can pick up the other two and cut over to the straight road. We have plenty of time. It's going to take them at least an hour to make it to Icebound Peak. But it's only a fifteen-minute drive."

"Zack, I hate to admit it," Slater said admiringly. "But sometimes that brain of yours does come in handy."

"That's *cervella* to you, *Signore* Slater," Zack said.

▲   ▼   ▲

When the gang got to Last Chance the next day, the Italians were talking to Denny outside of Vinnie's Place.

"Did you guys spot the car yet?" Denny asked them anxiously.

Zack shook his head. "Not a sign of it. How's the cesspool coming along?"

"Great," Denny said. "I'm done. Vinnie gave me the day off."

"Why don't you come with us, Denny?" Kelly suggested. "We're going to have a picnic at Icebound Peak."

"Yes, come," Francesco said. "We have plenty of food."

"But we don't have an extra bicycle," Antonio pointed out.

"That's okay," Denny said. "I'm not much

for bikes without motors, anyway. I'll drive up in Vinnie's car. I don't think my sister's bug would make it."

"Fantastic," Antonio said. "We'll probably get there around one-thirty."

"See you there. I'm going to go and cash in on my free breakfast," Denny said. He pushed open the door of the restaurant.

Zack couldn't believe it. Everywhere he turned this weekend, there was Denny Vane! He loved Kelly, but sometimes he wished that she wasn't *quite* so friendly. Why did she have to invite him?

"Ready?" Francesco asked the group.

Zack, Slater, and Screech gave their widest smiles. "Ready!" they chorused.

A half mile out of town, they hit the first hill. This time, Zack, Slater, and Screech didn't try to keep up. When they got to the top, the rest of the group had already gone around the next bend.

"Okay," Slater said. "I'm out of here. I'll meet you guys back here in twenty minutes, tops."

Zack and Screech wheeled their bicycles to the side of the road.

"Denny's a pretty nice guy," Screech observed. "I bet when he finally catches that guy, he lets him off with a warning."

"After he breaks his face," Zack said.

"What's a broken face compared with a broken conscience, Zack?" Screech asked solemnly.

"Screech, do you mind?" Zack said with a sigh. "I want to relax."

"No problemo," Screech said.

Zack stretched out on the grass, his hands behind his head. Now, *this* was the way to get to the top of a mountain, he thought, gazing up at a soft blue sky. The sun felt warm and the breeze stirred his hair. Before he knew it, Zack began to doze.

It didn't seem long at all before the toot of a car horn woke him up. Slater had pulled over and was waiting for them. But he wasn't in Mr. Belding's Toyota. He was in Zack's Mustang!

Chapter 9

▲ ▼ ▲ ▼ ▲

Slater got out of the car, a huge grin on his face. "Surprise!" he said. "I guess you're pretty glad to see this!"

"You bet," Zack gulped. "But how—?"

"Mr. Belding took his car somewhere," Slater explained as he opened the trunk to load in the bicycles. "I guess he got sick of fishing for nothing in the lake behind the house. So I gave the Mustang a try, and it started right up. Pretty weird, huh? I guess you've got a car that fixes itself, preppy."

"I guess so," Zack said. He looked at his watch. They still had plenty of time to get to Icebound Peak before Denny did. They were planning on hiding the car, anyway. So if Denny wasn't early, Zack'd be okay. But he sure didn't need the added aggravation!

Slater drove the car up the mountain road, following the curves easily. They reached Icebound Peak with time to spare. They pulled off into the small parking lot. On one side was a grassy meadow that overlooked a spectacular panoramic view of the valley below. On the other was a dense pine forest that was dwarfed by overcropping rocks.

"Where should we hide the car?" Slater asked.

Zack pointed to the opposite end of the parking lot. It sloped downward toward a small cluster of bushes. "There. If we drive across the grass a few feet, we can pull it behind those bushes."

Slater drove across the parking lot, bumped across the grass, and expertly maneuvered the car behind the bushes. When they got out and looked down from the parking lot, the car was completely concealed. They returned and lifted the bicycles from the trunk.

"Let's go to the meadow," Zack said. "We should be stretched out, relaxing, when they get here."

They left their bicycles in a bike rack in the parking lot and walked to the meadow. It was as beautiful as the Italians had promised, a lush green expanse spotted with wildflowers.

Zack got out his water bottle. He shook a few drops of water out and wet his hair and the front of his T-shirt.

"We should look a little sweaty," he advised.

Screech and Slater wet their hair and their T-shirts, too. Then they sat down on the grass to wait for the others.

When Francesco, Antonio, and Eugenio arrived, they looked shocked to see the boys. "But you're here already!" Francesco said.

"How did you go so fast?" Antonio asked.

Slater felt his calves. "It's the calf muscles," he said.

"It was a tough ride," Zack said. "But we managed it."

"How come you didn't pass us on the road?" Jessie asked suspiciously.

"We took the direct road," Slater said. "The other road is for wimps." He smiled at Antonio.

"Well, I must say, you made incredible time," Francesco said. Obviously, he suspected them of some sort of double-dealing. "You should be on the American Olympic team," he said jokingly.

Kelly looked at Zack suspiciously, but he only smiled innocently. "We sure worked up an appetite," he said.

Francesco tossed down his knapsack. "Okay, let's eat."

"*Mangia,*" Lisa translated, and Eugenio beamed at her. Angelica looked at Lisa with jealousy burning from her dark eyes.

Jessie poked Lisa. "You'd better watch out, girl," she murmured. "And we'd better keep the knives and forks away from Angelica."

Lisa tossed her head. "I'm not afraid of her."

"Then you're nuts," Jessie muttered. "I'm terrified."

Denny arrived just as Francesco handed out delicious sandwiches filled with Italian ham and fontina cheese. There were cookies and fruit for dessert. They ate every crumb and then wandered off in ones and twos to look at the view and explore the meadow. Everyone slowly straggled back to the blanket as the afternoon waned and the wind picked up.

Jessie tilted her head back and took a sip of water from her bottle. "I wish we had brought a thermos," she said. "It's cold up here. A cup of hot chocolate would be great."

Kelly nodded. "I'm glad we brought our sweatshirts."

"The elevation is pretty high," Zack said. He glanced up at the sky. "And it's getting cloudy."

Jessie shivered. "It feels like the temperature is really dropping."

"I have Uncle Vinnie's camper," Denny said. "I can give everyone a lift down the mountain, if you want. I think we'd all fit."

"Maybe that's not such a bad idea," Kelly said with a shiver.

Jessie nodded. "It sounds great. I'm freezing."

Francesco began to pack up the food. "I agree. I do not like the look of that sky."

"Where's Eugenio?" Antonio asked.

"I think he and Lisa went for a walk," Jessie said.

Antonio twisted around. "And where's Angelica?"

"She followed them, of course," Francesco said. "We will have to wait. They will be back soon, I am sure."

"Unless Angelica pushes Lisa off the mountain," Jessie whispered to Kelly.

▲   ▼   ▲

Lisa huddled closer to Eugenio. "It's getting colder," she said. "It sure doesn't feel like spring." She and Eugenio were hiking upward on a trail through the rocks. Eugenio had said that the view was even better a little higher up.

The sun had disappeared. And even though Lisa was wearing a thick sweatshirt, she was freezing.

Eugenio put his arm around her. "I will keep you warm."

Lisa smiled up at him. Eugenio's arm felt good, but she wasn't any warmer. Her teeth chattered a bit.

"You're really cold," Eugenio said in concern. "We will go back."

But Eugenio didn't move. He stood there, looking at her. "You are so delicate, Lisa. You are like a flower." He took her hands in his. "You are made for love and soft things, not rocks and mountains. I see you in a ballroom, in a beautiful gown."

"What color?" Lisa asked.

Eugenio laughed. "Spoken like a woman. Gold, I think."

"Perfect," Lisa said.

Eugenio kissed her hand. Lisa had never had her hand kissed before. She liked it. Maybe she could introduce the custom to the guys at Bayside High.

"I would like to protect you from everything ugly in life," Eugenio said. "I see you surrounded by beautiful things."

You should have seen me working in the hospital, Lisa thought. But, instead, she fluttered her eyelashes. "Oh, Eugenio," she said. "You're right. I'd like you to protect me."

This wasn't really her, Lisa thought. Only part of her was what Eugenio saw. Even she would get tired of gold gowns after a while. But Eugenio looked like he was about to kiss her, so she wasn't about to challenge him. His head bent toward hers, his dark eyes soft and shining....

"Hello!"

They heard the voice from behind them. Lisa stifled a groan. It was Angelica. Eugenio dropped her hand and looked behind them irritably.

In another moment, Angelica came into sight behind a curve. She waved at them. "I thought I heard you," she said.

"We were just heading back," Eugenio said with a frown.

"It's getting cold," Lisa said.

"I know an easier way to get down," Angelica said. "If you follow this a little and then take the right turning, you double back right into the meadow. Follow me." She started up the path ahead of them.

"But we're heading away from the meadow," Lisa said.

"The path doubles back in a minute," Angelica called.

"Are you sure she knows the way?" Lisa whispered to Eugenio as they followed Angelica.

He nodded. "She is the one who found this place. She has been up here at least a dozen times, exploring. I trust her."

Well, I don't, Lisa thought. But she pressed her lips together. Angelica was with them. Why would she get herself lost?

They walked faster, trying to warm up. Lisa's teeth started to chatter again. Suddenly, the trail opened up a bit. There was no sign of Angelica.

"Where is she?" Lisa asked.

"Probably around that bend," Eugenio said, speeding up. But when they rounded the bend, the trail was still empty. Ahead of them was a fork in the path. It was impossible to tell which path led down to the meadow.

"Angelica!" Eugenio called loudly. But they only heard the wind.

▲   ▼   ▲

The gang sat, wrapped in the picnic blankets, waiting for Eugenio, Lisa, and Angelica. Finally, they saw Angelica heading for them through the trees. She waved.

Jessie stood up. "Where are Lisa and Eugenio?"

"They went back down the mountain on their bikes," Angelica said. "They said they would meet us in town."

Kelly frowned. "That's strange," she said under her breath. It wasn't like Lisa to leave without telling them. But, then again, Lisa was capable of anything when a cute boy was involved.

"Well, then, we might as well go," Francesco said. "We will probably catch up to them on the drive back down."

On the way to the parking lot, Kelly checked the bike rack. Lisa and Eugenio's bicycles were gone, all right. Shrugging, she wheeled her bike to Denny's camper and loaded it in with the others.

Zack hung back with Slater and Screech. "Since we'll all fit in the camper, I guess we can leave the car," he said under his breath. "We don't want to blow our cover now. I'll think of something to tell Mr. Belding later, and he can drive me back up here to get it."

"What are you going to tell him?" Slater asked skeptically.

"Don't you have confidence in me?" Zack asked. "I'll think of something. What else are we going to do—confess that we drove up here and pretended to ride?"

"I guess not," Slater said grumpily. He wheeled his bike to Denny's camper.

On the drive down the mountain, everyone searched the road for Lisa and Eugenio, but there was no sign of them. They pulled into Last Chance, but Lisa and Eugenio weren't there, either. Everyone piled out of the car and looked up and down Main Street. Then everyone looked at Angelica.

"Are you *sure* they rode back down?" Jessie asked Angelica suspiciously.

Angelica tossed her thick, curly hair. "Of course I'm sure," she said.

Kelly brushed at her face. "I feel something," she said. She looked up at the sky. "Oh, my gosh!" she exclaimed. "It's *snowing!*"

It was true. A few flakes drifted down against the gray sky.

"Wow," Jessie said. "Snow in the springtime."

"It happens up here this late sometimes," Denny said, looking at the sky.

Zack frowned. "I'd hate to ride a bike down a mountain in it."

"I hope Lisa and Eugenio will be all right," Kelly said worriedly.

Even Angelica looked a little worried. "I am sure they will be fine," she said.

▲ ▼ ▲

"She took our bicycles!" Lisa exclaimed. "They're not here!"

"She probably hid them," Eugenio said. "It looks like she told the others that we had already gone."

"Eugenio, what are we going to do?" Lisa wailed. "I'm scared. It's getting darker and darker!"

"There, there, little flower," Eugenio said, slipping his arms around her and cradling her head against his chest. "I will protect you."

Lisa sniffed. She was freezing. She was thirsty. She was tired. Unless Eugenio planned on carrying her down the mountain, she didn't think there was much he could do.

"We will just go to the road and hitch a ride," Eugenio said. "Come on." He laced her fingers through his. "We will be back in Last Chance before you know it."

Lisa allowed herself to be led across the parking lot. It was nice to be taken care of, for a change. She'd been trained to handle emergencies. She probably could have figured out what to do on her own. But it was much nicer to be told. Besides, it got results. Eugenio was looking at her tenderly.

Suddenly, Lisa looked up at the sky. "Eugenio, look," she said. "It's snowing."

She saw Eugenio gulp as he looked at the sky. "Yes, it is," he said.

Lisa wanted to cry, but she was afraid her cheeks might freeze. Suddenly, the snow intensified. The flakes were thick and wet. She'd heard about freak blizzards in the mountains. They came on suddenly and fiercely, and they could be devastating. Lisa tried to be calm. If they could just get to the road, they could flag down a car.

"Hold on, Lisa," Eugenio said. "I think I see something." He went to the end of the parking lot and peered into the distance toward the ranger's hut. "I think I see metal. Angelica must have hidden our bikes in the bushes." He started down the slippery slope.

"But, Eugenio, we can't ride them, anyway," Lisa called after him. "Eugenio! It could be danger—"

Lisa's words were drowned out as Eugenio let out a cry. His arms flailed as his legs went out from underneath him as he fell and slipped down the incline.

"Oh, my gosh!" Lisa cried. She ran across the short distance and looked down the slope. Snow blew against her cheeks as she squinted down at

Eugenio. He lay at the bottom with his leg in a funny position.

"Are you okay?" she yelled.

"I do not think so," Eugenio shouted back weakly in a voice constricted with pain. "I think my leg might be broken."

Chapter 10

▲ ▼ ▲ ▼ ▲

Slipping and sliding, Lisa made her way quickly down the hill to Eugenio. His face was contorted in pain, and he was clutching his leg. She knelt by his side.

"Lisa," he moaned. "*Fa molto male.* It hurts very bad."

Although her heart was pounding, Lisa spoke in a quiet, calm voice. "Don't worry, Eugenio. You're going to be fine. I'll get you out of here. Now listen to me. Is it just your leg that hurts? Any pain in your back or your neck?"

He shook his head. "Just my leg."

"Your leg or your ankle?"

"My ankle," he said faintly.

"Okay, I'm just going to examine it. I won't hurt you." Remembering her first-aid training, Lisa felt Eugenio's leg and then moved on to his ankle. It was already starting to swell. She couldn't tell if it was a bad sprain or if it was broken. But that was a good sign. If it was a break, it wasn't a bad break. She'd have to leave his sneaker on. In this weather, his foot might freeze, and keeping the shoe on would contain the swelling a little bit. Lisa loosened the laces.

The snow blew against Lisa's cheeks as she thought rapidly. She slipped out of her sweatshirt and put it over Eugenio. Then she walked a few steps, looking at the ground. When she saw a big, flat rock, she picked it up with a grunt and brought it over. She laid it at Eugenio's feet.

"Okay, I'm just going to pick up your foot," she told him. "I'll try not to hurt you. We need to elevate your ankle to cut down on the swelling." Talking to him soothingly, Lisa picked up his foot and laid it gently down on the rock. Eugenio let out his breath in a hiss.

Lisa bent over him again. "I'm going to have to leave you," she told him. "I have to flag down a car. I don't want you to worry. It's not too cold, so there's no risk of exposure." That wasn't strictly true, but the less Eugenio knew, the better. The one thing Lisa was most afraid of was that he would go into shock. And without blankets, there was no way she could prevent it. She had to find help!

"I'll be right back," she repeated, gently smoothing his forehead.

He looked at her, glassy eyed, and tried to smile. "I will be okay."

Lisa struggled back up the hill. There had to be some traffic on the mountain road, she reasoned. Even though they were in a remote area, there still were people around, weren't there? And maybe the gang would start to worry about her soon.

Just as she reached the top of the hill, she saw Denny's camper pull into the parking lot. Lisa never was so happy to see anyone in her life. She waved at them frantically.

"They're here!" she yelled back down to Eugenio. Then she hurried toward the camper as Denny parked it.

"Lisa, you're here!" Kelly sprang out of the camper and ran toward her. "Angelica told us that you went back down the mountain."

"Luckily, she got scared when it started to snow," Jessie said.

"You guys, Eugenio is hurt," Lisa said breathlessly. "He fell down the slope and hurt his ankle. It might be broken. We have to get him to town."

From behind them, Angelica took a cautious step forward. Her face paled. "Eugenio?"

"That's right, Angelica," Lisa said crisply. "He was looking for our bicycles."

"Eugenio!" Angelica screamed, and started down the incline.

"Come on, guys," Lisa said to the gang. "We have to help Eugenio."

"We'd better hurry," Jessie said. "We listened to the radio on the way back up the mountain, and this storm is supposed to get worse."

The rest of the group followed Lisa. Angelica was already kneeling by Eugenio's side, tears pouring down her face. She sobbed to him in Italian.

"Tell Angelica to lighten up," Lisa said crisply to Francesco. "She isn't doing Eugenio any good. He has to stay calm."

Francesco spoke softly to Angelica in Italian, and Lisa turned to Zack, Slater, and Screech.

"Eugenio has to stay warm," she said in a low voice. "We've got to get him up to the camper. Try not to jolt him too much."

"That won't be easy," Slater said worriedly. "It's awfully slippery."

"We can do it," Lisa said. "We *have* to."

Zack exchanged a guilty look with Slater. It was time to confess. It was past time. It would be easier to transport Eugenio to the Mustang and then drive him to the camper. The car was hidden in the bushes not too far away. It was certainly better than trying to carry him.

"I think I have a better way," Zack told Lisa.

"What do you mean?" Lisa asked, looking worriedly at Eugenio.

Zack opened his mouth to tell her, but Screech suddenly threw himself on his knees in front of Denny.

"Please, please, don't kill him," he begged.

"He didn't mean to do it. It wasn't his fault. And you're a scary guy. That's why he couldn't tell you. But I know he would have sooner or later."

"What is he talking about?" Denny asked, looking around.

"Screech, how did you know?" Zack asked, astounded.

"I'm in the Chess Club, remember?" Screech said. "I saw the whole thing."

"Why didn't you say something?" Zack asked.

"Because I knew you had to make your own decision to tell," Screech said. "And I wouldn't tell Denny, even though he did threaten the entire chess club. You're my best friend, Zack."

"Wait a second," Denny said.

"Yeah, hold on," Jessie said. "Are you saying the Mustang is here?" She shot Slater a shrewd look. "So *that's* how you got up here so fast."

"Wait a second," Denny said.

"Yeah, wait a second," Kelly said. "Does that mean that *Zack's* the one who ran over Denny's bike?"

Suddenly, Denny's face assumed a homicidal expression. "You creep!" he roared. He sprang toward Zack, but he slipped in the snow and went down on one knee. "Ow," he said. Distracted, he started to rub it. "Now look what happened. Gee, Zack. I wasn't going to hurt you or anything."

"You guys," Lisa said, "you have to settle this later. We have to get Eugen—"

Lisa was stopped by the sound of tires against ice and gravel.

"What was that?" Slater asked, twisting around.

Denny rose to his feet. "It's the camper," he said, looking up at the parking lot. "It's moving."

Zack peered at it. "But who's driving it?"

"Nobody," Denny whispered. "I must have left it in gear."

He started toward it, but the camper was rolling faster now. The gang watched in horror as it rolled over the slippery snow, down the hilly parking lot toward the bushes to the left of them.

Denny ran as fast as he could, but the camper picked up speed. It bumped off the pavement and onto the grass. Then it rolled toward the bushes. It crashed through them with a snapping of branches. And then it crashed into something else.

For the second time that week, Zack heard the sickening crunch of metal against metal. Then there came a second, less noisy crash.

Zack closed his eyes. "There goes the Mustang," he said.

"Let's go check the damage," Slater said.

Lisa and the Italians stayed with Eugenio, and the rest of the group trudged over to where the smashed cars sat.

"It looks bad," Zack said, checking out the Mustang. The camper had pushed it a few feet into a pine tree. "As a matter of fact, I think it's totaled."

"The camper looks worse," Denny said, surveying it.

"You'd better see if they're drivable," Slater advised.

Zack and Denny crawled into their damaged vehicles and tried to start them up. Neither engine would start. Slater tried to pop the hoods of both cars, but they were both crunched too badly.

Zack looked at the gang through the blowing snow. "What are we going to do? We've got to get Eugenio out of here—not to mention ourselves. The snow is getting worse."

"This is a disaster," Kelly said, shivering.

"I'm scared," Jessie said. She drew closer to Slater, and he put his arm around her. Even though Antonio was fun, Slater made her feel safe.

"We'd better tell Lisa," Zack said.

They trudged back through the snow to Lisa and told her the bad news. Angelica began to wail, and Francesco looked angry. He let loose a stream of Italian.

"I think he's blaming us for this mess," Zack said.

Kelly looked at him. "If the shoe fits."

"Hey, it wasn't Zack's fault," Slater said.

"No, it was *all* of yours," Jessie said, moving away from Slater's arm. "If you guys hadn't tried to play a trick on us, Denny's camper wouldn't be trashed."

"Wait a second. Denny's camper still would have rolled into the trees," Slater pointed out.

"But if you hadn't hidden the Mustang, Lisa and Eugenio would have had a car up here," Kelly said.

"No, we would have driven it down the mountain," Zack said.

"Let us face it," Antonio said. "It is Angelica's fault. She is the one who told us that Eugenio and Lisa had left."

"It's all your fault," Denny told her.

A fresh flood of tears burst forth from Angelica. "*Non capisco,*" she said, looking from one face to another.

"How do you like that," Denny said. He turned to the others. "All of a sudden, the chick can't speak English."

Angelica wiped her cheeks. "I didn't know it would snow. I just wanted to punish him. I would have come back to get them."

Then everyone started to talk at once. Panicked and scared, they just wanted to blame each other.

Suddenly, Lisa stood up. "That's enough!" she yelled. Everyone stopped talking and looked at her. "This is not productive," she said crisply. "We have decisions to make."

Angrily, she led the group a little ways from Eugenio. She turned to Denny. "Does your uncle actually use that camper for camping?"

Denny nodded. "All year long. He's a nature freak."

"Then you and Screech go back and see what you can find. Sleeping bags, maybe a kerosene heater. Any food. And try to find matches! Oh, and see if he has emergency flares, too."

"Yes, sir," Denny said, and he and Screech took off.

"Slater, do you think you could carry Eugenio to the camper?" Lisa asked. "It's not too smashed up to sit in, is it?"

Slater shook his head. "I think we can all fit in the back if we squeeze in," he said.

"Just be careful of his ankle," Lisa said. "I'll come with you. We need to find a pillow, or something soft, to rest his foot on. We've got to keep the ankle elevated. Jessie, come with me and Slater and help us get Eugenio settled in the camper. We have to get him out of the cold."

She turned to Zack. "Zack, you and Kelly come, too. We'll try to find any extra sweatshirts and T-shirts. You guys can put them on and then hike to the road and see if you can flag down a car. If we have flares, plant them so that they're pointing to the parking lot. Don't stay outside longer than fifteen minutes. We don't want anyone getting pneumonia if we can help it."

"What can we do, Lisa?" Francesco asked.

Lisa frowned. "There's that little ranger station on the other side of the parking lot. See if you can break in through a window. This is an emergency. There might be a radio in there."

Francesco nodded, and he and Antonio moved off.

"What can I do?" Angelica asked, wiping at her face.

"Stop crying," Lisa advised. "Keep talking to Eugenio and try to take his mind off this."

"You are wonderful, Lisa," Angelica said. "So brave. I do not know what we would have done—"

"Save it for when we get off the mountain," Lisa said bluntly. Then, as Angelica moved away and she was alone, she clenched her hands together so that they'd stop shaking. "If we ever do," she whispered to herself.

Chapter 11

▲ ▼ ▲ ▼ ▲

Following the beam of an electric torch, Zack and Kelly trudged across the parking lot to the road. The darkness had fallen fast. Now it was almost impossible to see in the pitch black and through the driving snow.

They had left Lisa giving orders. Eugenio was now lying in back of the camper, snug and warm in a sleeping bag with his foot propped up on a knapsack. Lisa had even found two aspirins to give to him.

Denny had had his weekend bag in the camper, and his uncle had had several sweatshirts balled up in the back. Lisa had distributed the clothing. Kelly was now wearing Denny's motorcycle jacket, and Zack had scored Uncle Vinnie's old sweatshirt, which smelled of campfire smoke and fish.

Zack sneaked a look at Kelly's profile. Even in the darkness, he could tell that she was still angry at him. He didn't know where to start or what to say. Sometimes it seemed like he was always trying to explain to Kelly why he had acted like an idiot. Maybe because he *was.* He had stretched the truth, cut corners, or tried to wiggle out of wrongdoings more times than he could count. And Kelly had always been there to sigh in disappointment or be angry or give him a lecture. But she had always forgiven him.

Had he finally pushed her too far? Had she finally run out of forgiveness?

"Kelly—" he started.

"Don't, Zack," Kelly said. "Don't start telling me all the reasons you did what you did."

"But—"

"I've heard it all before, more times than I can count," Kelly said. "All the reasons why you had to tell one little white lie, or stretch the truth, or keep something from me. Sooner or later, I have to face up to the fact that I'm stupid. I keep *listening* to you. And you keep promising to be honest with me. And then you end up hurting me again."

"But, Kelly," Zack said, "I didn't lie to you. I just didn't tell you about Denny's motorcycle. Actually, I—"

Kelly stopped short and faced him. "That's just the trouble, Zack," she said, swiping at a lock of hair that blew against her cheek. "You think that not telling me something means that you're still being honest."

"Well, at least I didn't *lie*," Zack said.

Kelly started to walk again. "Okay, just for the sake of argument, let's look at the situation. You didn't tell me about running over Denny's bike."

"Just a little omission of fact," Zack said.

"But you had to hide your car, so you told me it was broken. Was that true, Zack? Or was it a lie?"

"Oh," Zack said. "I see what you mean."

"And *because* you told me that lie, when Jean-Marie saw you buying ice cream with some girl the other night and told me, I got upset."

"I was with my mother!"

"How was I supposed to know that? Okay, let's take the next point. You broke a date with me and said you had to study. But when I called you that night—"

"—I didn't know you called me that night!"

"—your mother said you were out."

"I was out in the garage trying to soak off that darn green bumper sticker," Zack explained. "But I couldn't tell you because—"

"Because you never told me that you ran over Denny's bike," Kelly finished. "Instead, you said that your car was still in the shop, and that was why you couldn't drive me to school or see me. But when I went to your house and looked in your garage window, there was your car."

Zack moaned. But there was nothing he could say.

"So all week long, I was thinking that you were seeing another girl." They reached the road, and Kelly turned to him. "Tell me something, Zack. Was it worth it to you? Was it worth hurting me like that?"

"Kelly, nothing is worth hurting you," Zack said steadily. His heart throbbed with pain.

"Then why do you keep doing it, Zack?" Kelly asked. He could hear the unshed tears in her voice.

It was dark and windy on the road. Snow caught like diamonds in Kelly's dark hair. Her blue eyes sparkled, but with tears, not happiness.

"Because I don't deserve you," Zack said. "Because I'm not as good as you, or as good as you want me to be. But I love you more than anything in the world, Kelly."

Kelly stuck a flare in the ground by the entrance to the parking lot. "You know what the funny thing is, Zack? If you had told me, none of this would have happened. And you would have been okay with Denny, too. You guys think he's a tough hood with a bad attitude. But girls know better. He's just a marshmallow."

"Well," Zack said. "I don't know about *that.*"

"Not only don't you trust me, you don't trust my judgment, either," Kelly said.

"That's not true, Kelly," Zack said desperately. "I just happen to believe a guy in motorcycle boots when he says he wants to stomp my face in."

"You know what's funny?" Kelly mused. "Back there, when Denny found out you'd been the hit-and-run driver, you never once said you were sorry. And I was just thinking. You never said it to me, either. Why is it so hard for you to say you're sorry, Zack?"

Snow blew against Zack's cheeks, stinging them. "I don't know," he said helplessly.

She turned away. "We'd better set the flares," she said.

"Wait, Kelly. Are you saying you can't forgive me?" Zack asked. His heart seemed to stop beating while he waited for Kelly's answer.

"No, Zack, I can forgive you," she said slowly. A tear slowly trickled down her cold, pale cheek. "I just don't know if I can love you anymore."

▲   ▼   ▲

When they got back to the camper, everything had been organized by Lisa. She had flipped down the middle seat to make more room, and distributed the three sleeping bags and two blankets among the group. They looked almost cozy by the tiny light of the camper when Zack and Kelly opened the door.

"Hurry and come in," Lisa said. "The wind is freezing. Did you set the flares?"

Zack and Kelly crawled into the camper. "All set," Zack said. "Any luck at the ranger station?"

Francesco shook his head. He was huddled in a blanket with Antonio and Angelica. "They are not open for the season, so there is no radio or anything. The place was bare."

"Here, guys," Lisa said. "We saved this sleeping bag for you to share."

Zack unzipped the bag and waited while Kelly crawled in. Then he squeezed in next to her. He could feel how stiff and anxious she was. Zack felt awful. If they ever got off this mountain, he'd have to think of a way to get her back. But Zack felt despair at the thought. This was the worst fight they had ever had.

Jessie shivered and moved closer to Slater. "It's so dark," she said.

"And windy," Angelica said.

"Well, we have one consolation at least," Slater said. "We don't have to eat Mr. Belding's cooking tonight."

Everyone laughed weakly. Then Jessie moaned. "Oh, I wish you hadn't mentioned food," she said.

"This will be some story to tell the kids at the hospital," Denny said. "After reading to them from books, I finally have my *own* story to tell."

"Denny reads to the little kids at the hospital twice a week," Lisa explained to the others.

Funny. Zack had forgotten all about that. And he'd been the one to come up with the idea in the first place. The gang had practically blackmailed Denny into volunteering, after they'd realized that Denny had been the one to steal the senior class fund and then replace it.

"Denny, do you have any books with you by any chance?" Lisa asked.

"As a matter of fact, I do," Denny said. "I was at the hospital before I headed for Last Chance. Francesco, could you hand me that backpack?"

Francesco passed over the knapsack he was leaning against. Denny fished through it. "Whoa, I have some of my favorites here," he said. "How about *Buddy the Bear's Big Day*? It's my favorite story, guys. You're going to love it."

"Read on," Lisa said. She checked Eugenio's ankle to make sure there wasn't any discoloration from the swelling. If she saw some, she'd loosen his sneaker more. He smiled at her weakly. She fervently hoped a story, even a children's story, would relax him a little bit.

Slater held a flashlight over Denny's shoulder. Denny cracked open the book, cleared his throat, and began to read. His voice had a soft, lulling effect, as he told the story of a mischievous baby bear. He chuckled along with the funny parts and grew anxious at the scary parts. He held the group spellbound. They could almost forget the howling wind and blowing snow outside.

When he finished Buddy's story, he started on *Rumpelstiltskin*. Next to him, Zack could feel Kelly slowly begin to relax. But every time she began to lean against him comfortably, she straightened and leaned the opposite way, against the back of the front seat.

"That was great, Denny," Jessie said when he'd finished.

"*Magnifico*," Francesco agreed.

"How's Eugenio?" Kelly asked.

Lisa smiled. "He's asleep. I think he dropped off near the end. Sleep is the best thing for him."

"If I could just stop thinking about food," Jessie groaned.

"Please," Slater said. "Don't mention the word. I can't believe we ate that whole picnic lunch. There wasn't even a crumb left."

"Do not say the word *crumb*," Antonio said. "I would kill for one."

"Denny," Lisa said, "can you read us another story?"

"You bet," Denny said happily. "I've got *The Ballards of Runneymeade*—that's about this totally cool family of mice. And I have *Puss 'n' Boots*. A classic."

"I vote for the mice," Screech said.

"*Puss 'n' Boots*," Slater argued.

"I think the first one," Francesco said.

The girls giggled. "I never thought I'd see the day," Jessie said, rolling her eyes. "Guys arguing over fairy tales."

"Shhhh," Lisa said suddenly. "I hear something."

Everyone fell silent and strained their ears. Sure enough, after a moment they heard the crunch of wheels on snow.

"It's a car!" Slater said. He was leaning against the side door, and he opened it. Screech, who had also been leaning against it, tumbled out.

"We're over here!" he called, upside down.

They saw the wavering light of a flashlight, and a moment later, a state trooper poked his head into the camper.

"You kids stuck?"

"We sure are," Zack said. "And we have an injured person here."

"His ankle might be broken," Lisa said, as Eugenio woke with a groan.

"Okay," the trooper said. "Sit tight. I'll radio for help."

In just a few minutes, there were two four-wheel-drive vehicles in the parking lot. Eugenio was bundled into the first one.

"Lisa!" he called weakly. "Can you come with me to the hospital?"

"Of course I'm coming," Lisa assured him. She held his hand tightly. "I wouldn't leave you now."

"And can you do something else for me?" he whispered.

"Anything," she promised.

"Can you ask if Angelica can ride with us, too?"

"Angelica?" Lisa asked, surprised. "But, Eugenio, she's the reason you're hurt. She lied because she was jealous."

"I know," he said. A smile spread over his pale face. "Now I realize how much she loves me after all."

Chapter 12

▲　▼　▲　▼　▲

The state trooper's car was full of a happy, laughing crew as they drove slowly back down the mountain. Everyone was relieved that Eugenio was finally safe and on his way to a doctor. And everyone was really looking forward to something to eat!

"It's almost ten o'clock," Slater said. "I've *never* gone this long without eating. Even Mr. Belding's food is going to look good."

"You might have gone longer without eating if your friend Mr. Belding hadn't alerted us that you were missing," the state trooper said. "He was mighty worried. And a Mr. Fellini was talking so fast I couldn't understand a word he was saying."

"That is our coach," Antonio explained.

"Anyway, the two fellas are holed up in the Wintergreen cabin, waiting and worrying. You kids scared them half to death."

"Uh-oh," Zack said. "Mr. Belding will probably suspend us now."

"And Coach Fellini will drop us from the team," Francesco said.

But when the gang arrived at the cabin, they were greeted with hugs and handshakes and a roaring fire.

"All of a sudden, this is the most luxurious place I've ever seen!" Jessie said, laughing.

The smell of something delicious permeated the warm cabin, and the gang sniffed the air, their stomachs rumbling.

"As soon as we heard you were safe, Marcello drove back to where they were staying and brought back some groceries," Mr. Belding said, beaming. "He's got pasta on the stove and chicken in the oven."

"I can't wait," Slater said.

Mr. Belding pointed toward the living room. "And there's some hard sausage and cheese in front of the fire. Go in and get warm. I'll bring in some sodas."

"This is so great," Jessie said, pulling an armchair close to the fire and sinking into it. She leaned forward and grabbed a cracker and a piece of cheese.

"I thought I would never be warm again," Francesco said, rubbing his hands together.

"What a day!" Antonio said, laughing. "We wanted to spend it alone in a mountain meadow with three beautiful American girls, and we end up stuck on a mountaintop in a storm."

"Alone?" Slater asked suspiciously. "So you did want to steal our girls!"

"Of course," Francesco said, beaming. "We're Italian."

"And your girls are *bellissima*," Antonio said, kissing his fingers to Jessie and Kelly.

"But you guys showed us," Francesco said, laughing. "Driving your car up the mountain. That was good!"

"We would have done the same thing," Antonio confessed, and everyone burst out laughing.

Zack led Denny away to a corner of the room. "Listen, Denny," he said awkwardly. "I'm sorry about hitting your bike. And I'm sorry I didn't tell you. I can't believe I'm saying this to a guy who just read me fairy tales. But, Denny, you *scare* people."

"I do?" Denny said. "I'm just trying to get my point across."

"Well, Screech was right about something. I would have confessed, sooner or later. The guilt was driving me crazy." *And driving my girlfriend away*, he thought.

Denny shrugged. "Yeah, well, it's all water over the bridge. And it was my fault that your Mustang got totaled. Maybe we should just call it even. I mean, we both destroyed each other's favorite form of transportation, right?"

"True," Zack said, and they shook hands. He

was hoping that Kelly saw it, but when he looked over, she was talking to Francesco and didn't see him at all.

▲   ▼   ▲

After everyone had eaten their fill of spaghetti and roast chicken, they took turns calling their parents to let them know they were safe. Even though Mr. Belding had called them, the gang knew their parents would worry if they didn't hear from their children personally.

The storm began to subside when Coach Fellini and the Italians headed off to the hospital to check on Eugenio. Denny hitched a ride to town with them in order to face the music with his uncle Vinnie. Mr. Belding insisted on doing the dishes. Screech went off to take a hot shower, and Jessie and Slater went out to get a breath of fresh air. That left Zack and Kelly alone.

"You'd think those two would have had enough fresh air today," Zack observed as he settled into an armchair on the opposite side of the fireplace from Kelly.

"I think they want to be alone for a while," Kelly said, watching the flames. "Slater was jealous of Antonio, and Jessie wanted to reassure him."

"They're lucky," Zack said. But Kelly didn't

say anything. She just looked at the flames as though the secret to life was written in them. Zack knew he had to use his last resort—honesty.

Suddenly, he realized why Kelly was so angry and disappointed in him. Usually, honesty *was* his last resort. But when he was wrong or uncertain or just plain scared, honesty was a hard route to take.

"Kelly, I'm sorry," he said. "They should have been the first words out of my mouth, to you and Denny. I know it's too late to say them. But I really feel them."

"It is too late, Zack," Kelly said with a sigh. "But I appreciate your saying them."

"Look," he said. "I know you don't want to talk to me right now."

"That's very perceptive of you, Zack."

"Then you can just listen," Zack said firmly. "I've been thinking, Kelly. When you knew for sure that my car wasn't broken, why didn't you tell me that you knew?"

For the first time since they'd talked up on the mountaintop, Kelly looked at him. "What?"

"Why didn't you tell me that you knew I'd lied, that you thought I was seeing someone else?" Zack persisted.

"Because I couldn't," Kelly said. "I was too hurt. I didn't want to talk about it."

"So you weren't honest with me."

Kelly tossed her head, her eyes flashing. "It's

not the same thing, Zack. Don't turn this on me."

"I'm not trying to." Zack got up and crossed the distance between them. "What I'm trying to say," he said gently, "is that we all find it hard to be honest sometimes. Even you, when the stakes are high enough. When you feel too much. Kelly, I know it seems like I hide things from you or cut corners just so I can escape responsibility. And that's definitely *part* of it. But the biggest part of it is that I'm scared."

Kelly looked at him searchingly. "What do you mean, Zack? Scared of what?"

"Scared of losing you," Zack said. "Scared of being such a messed-up guy that you'll say forget it. I think that's why I have a problem saying I'm sorry. Like if I admit that I'm wrong, you'll realize it, too. And I'll lose you."

"Oh, Zack," Kelly said. Tears started to slip down her cheeks. "I don't care if you mess up sometimes. I just want you to share it with me. I don't want to find out from someone else or from peeking in a window. I want to find out from *you.*"

Zack looked at the faded carpet for a minute. "I've said this so many times before," he said. "I'm embarrassed to say it again. But, Kelly, I've never meant it more. I'll be better. Now I realize that just loving you isn't enough. You're right. I have to trust you and also trust myself enough to be honest with you. Kelly, I'll try to be the best person I can be for you."

"That's all I've ever wanted," Kelly said softly. "Zack, I don't want to turn you into a straight-arrow type of guy. I just want you to let me in. I want you to trust me." She slipped her hand into his, and her small fingers curled around his.

"I want you to trust me to keep on loving you," she said.

Zack looked into her eyes. Love looked back at him, shining, clear. Love he could trust in. "I do," he said.

▲   ▼   ▲

When Lisa returned a half hour later, the gang was gathered by the fire, finishing the night off with cups of hot cocoa.

"How's Eugenio?" everyone asked at the same time.

"He's going to be fine," Lisa said, taking off her sweatshirt. "He has a fractured ankle, and he'll have to wear a cast for a while. But the doctors say he can start training again in only a few months."

"That's a relief," Jessie said, and everyone nodded.

Lisa grinned. "And it looks like he and Angelica are an item again."

"Oh, Lisa, I'm sorry," Jessie said. "Are you okay?"

"Are you kidding? I'm relieved," Lisa admitted with a whoop. "Let me tell you, it was *tiring* fluttering my eyelashes while riding a bicycle up a mountain."

Everyone laughed, and Lisa held out her hands to the fire.

"That feels so good," she said. "I don't think I've warmed up yet."

"Here, Lisa, take my seat," Screech said, jumping up. "I'll pour you a cup of cocoa. You deserve to be waited on."

"You're our hero," Jessie said.

"If it weren't for Lisa, Mr. Belding, we would have fallen apart," Kelly said. "She told us to stop blaming each other and deal with the situation."

"She got us all organized," Zack agreed. "We never would have thought of looking for those flares without her."

"She knew just what to do for Eugenio," Slater said. "It was very impressive."

"And she's the one who thought of getting Denny to read to us," Jessie said. "That really calmed our nerves. And it was great for Eugenio. He even fell asleep!"

"Cut it out, you guys," Lisa said, blushing. "You're embarrassing me. I just did what I had to do."

"But you knew exactly what to do," Zack said. "You really learned a lot being a candy striper. We never gave you enough credit."

"Even when you saved that little boy," Jessie said. "We just thought it was luck."

"We're sorry, Lisa," Kelly said. "We've been talking about it, and we feel badly. We really underestimated you."

Lisa took a cup of cocoa from Screech with a smile. "Hey, I underestimated *myself*," she said wryly. "I didn't need you guys to do it for me. I'm the champ when it comes to messing up."

"Hey, I already have that title," Zack said with a groan, and everybody laughed. "I should have admitted to Denny right away that I ran over his bike. I should have been honest with him—and with all of you." *Especially you,* his eyes told Kelly.

"That's right, Zack," Mr. Belding said. "I hope you learned your lesson."

"Please, Mr. Belding," Slater said. "We're not in school today. Do we *have* to learn lessons?"

Everybody laughed, even Mr. Belding. "I hate to tell you this, A. C., but it's Monday," he said. "The clock just struck midnight."

"Well, *I* don't mind learning a lesson," Lisa said. "I learned that I have to be honest with myself. I like medicine and I'm good at it. I'm going to pursue both it *and* fashion. There's still plenty of time to make a choice. And if being really deep and being really superficial at the same time is a contradiction, so what?" Lisa shrugged her shoulders. "That's me."

"That's a good lesson," Kelly agreed. "We

shouldn't listen too much to what other people think of us. We should just follow our hearts."

"And our consciences," Zack added, with a special smile for Kelly.

Jessie nodded. "It's important for us all to be ourselves."

"You said it," Slater said.

Mr. Belding rolled his eyes. "And heaven help the rest of us," he said. "Now that I've spent a weekend with you guys, I know how wild it can get."

Screech nodded, his frizzy curls bobbing. "I know what you mean, Mr. Belding," he said. "But at least Flora and Fauna never showed up!"